Passage from Home

Philip Callow

Passage from Home

A Memoir

Shoestring Press

Typeset and printed by Q3 Print Project Management Ltd, Loughborough, Leicestershire.
(01509 213456)

Published by Shoestring Press
19 Devonshire Avenue, Beeston, Nottingham, NG9 1BS
(0115) 925 1827
www.shoestringpress.co.uk

First published 2002
© Copyright: Philip Callow
ISBN: 1 899549 65 X

east | **midlands**
arts
making creative
opportunities

Shoestring Press gratefully acknowledges financial assistance from East Midlands Arts

The Critics on Philip Callow

"His prose is clear and easy and elegant, his observation sharp but kind and never superficial."

— V.S. NAIPAUL

"By some happy balance of insight and sympathy, Philip Callow manages to engage attention and understanding without alienating common sense. His achievement is to let us see impulses and passions from the inside, without censure or praise."

— MARGARET DRABBLE

"There is an aroused, never quite defined current of emotion running under the prose which ensures that the story, however familiar by now, remains constantly readable."

— A. ALVAREZ

"Philip Callow ... is a born writer, every one of whose paragraphs is shaped with conscious artistry."

— FRANCIS KING

"Callow has a voice which is very much his own: he shows not just intense nervous energy but what seems to be painful nerve ends, an oppenness to feeling, to suffering and joy at simple, almost primitive levels. What moves him moves the reader. The slant of the world seems his; he has a hold on nature, on the root of feeling."

— ISABEL QUIGLY

"Callow's writing is like nothing but itself, tense, uneasy, sometimes with a clean lift as if the words had not been used before, never without its own nervous integrity."

— ANGELA CARTER

Author's Note

The material from a few pages of my early collection of short stories, *Native Ground*, has been rewritten and included in this memoir.

To my friend
Jim Morgan

Chapter 1

They are a tiny enclosed world of three adults and two boys, in what would now be called an inner-city street. "Hold his hand," his mother orders him, the older boy, when they go out on Saturday nights with their deaf grandfather, and until they are out of sight round the first corner he does. "Up the town," his grandfather calls it, and it is truly uphill, a steep climb all the way. The little man he thinks of as old always calls in at a poky off-license for his ruby wine, where they fill his bottle on draught from a great swelling barrel high on a shelf. He remembers the wooden tap. But surely not ruby red: never red. No, it is tawny brown. The bottle wrapped in newspaper slips into his grandfather's oilskin shopping bag. What it tastes like God knows, because it must be cheap. If they had allowed him to sip it he would have wanted to spit it out like medicine. He is ten, his brother six. They are on their Saturday night treat, past eight at night and all the shops busy as ever: eager for ice-cream in a tin dish upstairs in Woolworth's cafeteria. Tin dish with a dent in it: the tin spoon. Nectar of the gods.

He likes the winter nights best, the exciting blaze of shops in the dark overhanging streets clogged with shoppers, the acetylene flares that blow and hiss on the stall corners of the market in the cold wind, dense throngs treading in mud and trampled rubbish on the beaten ground. His grandfather is on the forage for bargains, with the market closing, traders impatient to leave. "Go on then, 'ave this cabbage with them carrots," and into his capacious bag go the bargains. He is known in the market, and by men of his age who come up and bawl, "Orl right, Ted?" in his ear, and he nods and grins. They slap his back and go on.

Heading for home there are detours. This is the night for his sick clubs, tuppence here, fourpence there, meagre provisions for a time when he might fall ill or get sacked. In the frosty light of stone church rooms where a man sits drearily at a trestle table, entering the pittance on his grubby card, either saying nothing or "Ted". The old man waits in silence and they stand behind him. Back home he unwraps his ruby wine and tips his bargains on the kitchen table from splitting carrier bags. "Good lord, now what have you got?" cries his daughter, full in his face, and he feels sorry that his grandfather's moment of triumph is ruined. But clearly he doesn't care or mind. "Usual load of rubbish," mutters his son-in-law, half hidden behind his newspaper. "Hush, Hubert," his wife scolds.

Coming home in the dark streets with its black shadows he draws close to his grandfather as he feels the bristle of menace in the air, a drunk reeling out of a pub red with spilled light, paintwork a frenzied green, inside the bedlam of catcalls, wild laughter and shrieks. Bedraggled women stranded on the wet pavement, one with a pram. Near the bottom of the hill at the base of the enormous black cliff of the Morris building is a cut-through that runs straight as a slot between blank factory walls and shoots you out on Gulson Road. It scares him but in daylight he finds the nerve to race through very fast as if sucked along. On its corner is a stone mason's yard behind railings, cluttered with tombstones and winged angels covered in dust. They call the passage Shut Lane but it should be shit lane, because people come to empty their dogs down it.

This is their district, and their street of terraced houses flush on the pavement a hundred yards in length, fleapit cinema at one end and newsagent at the other could be called a slum street – outside lavatories, dirt entries, two up two down hovels, the galvanised coffin of a bath on a hook in the yard. But a tidy, law-abiding slum. Most of the tenants quiet and inoffensive like his family, except for the poor mad woman barricaded behind her front door at number 48 whom you were warned about, and the glaring giantess halfway down in a shawl and a man's cap, brawny arms crossed over her pinny. She stands like a sentry on her doorstep in her men's boots and you are told never to stare as you go past. And for his first seven years he thinks that this is how everyone lives. No, he doesn't think. It is his world, it glows at its core like the cast-iron black-leaded range they cook on and warm themselves at, and the glow is his mother, her anxious love; a mother unwilling to comprehend that he is not her.

Conscious life begins for him in 32 Vecqueray Street, Coventry. His first memory is a dim, mysterious one, strange as a dream. Does it really happen or has he been told it did? He is four, playing in the street, and the handlebar grip of a passing motorbike catches him on the side of the head. Knocked out, he comes round in the front room of a slovenly house in the street, craning faces asking who he is. Years later he remembers the circle of strange, examining women. Always these caring, selfless women, starting with his own mother. Next comes Miss Allen, tall and straight as a queen, first teacher of his Infants class. But his grandmother is the one, mother of his father, such an old, soft dumpling of a creature with her dense flood of silver hair loosed in the night, wrapping him in her old arms after a nightmare and saying "there" over and over. With her three awkward, bony sons, all obstinate in their different ways, her morose, dark-eyed daughter and her starchy railway-guard husband with his thick moustache who comes back after days away in all the glory of his uniform, his gold-braided cap, watch-chain and furled flags, the red and the green, the whistle that he would take out solemnly and inspect. He remembers his grandmother's sweet floury smell, his guard-grandfather's distance.

His mother's father has moved in to 32 after his wife's death and is now permanent: the old man, or old pot and pan, called Old Pot for short. His father's dislike of this arrangement is obvious to them all To placate the head of the household the old man addresses him as "boss". "All right, boss?" Is it a cunning form of mockery? Safe behind a stone-deaf wall of silence. His grandson thinks of him as old, but the o-p is no more than sixty. Short as his mother but a compact, labourer's body. His heavy Victorian moustache filters the tea he sucks up from his saucer. A genial, smelly old man who saves up for his grandchildren in a Christmas Club toyshop: behind his hooded, ringed eyes a smouldering temper that has been damped down by the years. When he is safely dead his daughter writes down her girlhood memories in her looping hasty hand, capitals falling backwards and a dearth of punctuation, sentences running together and her father

3

looming out as a short-legged, tin-pot tyrant terrifying on Saturday nights when the pubs empty, children and mother huddled together upstairs in their slum court as the lord and master crashes in through the door. Once in his cups he staggered in with a live pig he had won in a raffle. Now he sits diminished and watchful in his own cracked leatherette armchair, head bowed over his Edgar Wallace, encased in the stillness of a premature old age as he eyes the enemy over taped specs. "Eh?" he would answer any question from his daughter, making her work and shout. "What's that, boss?" he counters his son-in-law's wrath, not so much respectful as defensive.

His father, back erect from his army training, the steady provider for them all, even through the Depression, towering over his small mother, high and thin, goes off muttering that the old devil can hear him alright if he chooses. All through his childhood he never once hears his father swear: not that he is churchy. And he is tested enough. If the o-p suddenly passes out in an insulin coma, or thrashes about upstairs in a diabetic fit, his father hurls himself up the narrow stairs to hold him down on the bed, something he doesn't see, but the commotion fills the tiny house with violence. None of it is spoken about. The wild beating of his terror-filled heart subsides, and next day it is as if it has never been. The old rampaging bull gelded, inert again in his armchair.

Easy to remember is the morning ritual, the o-p being given his insulin jab in his upper arm, and no doubt the needles are often not sharp enough. Shirt-sleeve rolled back, he sits at the kitchen table and his mother strikes, dabbing clumsily afterwards with a bit of cotton wool because what comes next always unnerves her. "Cruel bitch!" he swears at her, perhaps worse if they are alone, if there is no witness. Then the ritual of bandaging his arms with strips of cloth for protection at work – he lowers components into acid tanks at a ramshackle chromium plating shop in Godiva Street nearby. There the o-p is six days a week, and when his grandson calls with his forgotten sandwiches he is out of sight somewhere in the sharp stink and the clouds of steam. "Ted!" they yell into the murk, a weedy youth is sent with a message, then out of the cave of choking steam clumps his grandfather dressed as a warrior, unrecognisable almost, a sort of bonnet round his head, enormous rubber gloves the colour of mustard, rubber apron, rubber boots. Grinning, with the youth watching. The boy knows him by his short legs, stumpy figure, dragging off a glove to mumble "Ta." Takes the packet and retreats backwards, disappears, steam falling like a curtain. The sight gives him a pang and he runs off forlorn, as if he grasps somehow what it is like, the fate of a semi-literate labouring man forced to sell his time, do anything.

All ritual. It all goes with home, with family. So do the visits of Cyril, a favourite uncle, making reluctantly for his night shift at the Standard Motor Company. He is an auto setter, always sleepy and bleary-eyes, his hands gloved invisibly with an ointment to ward off the suds oil that cascades over the tools of his autos. He is shy, slow, dreamy, he rakes through his hair with thin fingers, his glances indirect; yawning. The yawn turns into a smile aimed at his mother. His nephew wonders at his uncle's upside-down life. He wipes his mouth on the back of his hand and sits on a hard chair near the door, not staying, passing through. Only he always settles himself and stays, hangs on, lingers. Addressing his nephew like a man, he asks, "How's it going?" Proudly, pleased, the boy answers in a gruff manner that seems to him appropriate, "Not bad, thanks."

His father disapproves of Cyril's lethargic attitude, his time-wasting. Lethargic he certainly is. Unmarried, living with that grandmother the boy adores so much. Who could leave such a treasure? Not him, he's too comfortable, a born lingerer. Mother brings his cup of tea and he ducks his nose to it and talks softly, saying little, looking perfectly at home, making her laugh. Just the look of him. He appears, then the laughter comes. Lifting the steaming liquid in spoonfuls at first, fastidious, blowing carefully. His legs crossed, tucked under his chair

"A bachelor trick, that," his mother says.

"What is?" he asks mildly.

"What you're doing."

"Go on."

"It's true."

"No."

"Laugh then," his mother says, "You'll see." Predicting something that comes true.

His mother, the terrible worrier who seldom laughs, burdens weighing on her, laughs when he comes. This for him is Cyril's great achievement, coaxing laughs from his mother. His heart lifts when he sees her happy.

Why should Cyril be the favourite uncle? Perhaps because he senses he is a lone spirit, free to wander in and out, not shackled to duties like the others. Soon a kind of unacknowledged chum sits in their cramped living room, part of the family almost, whether his father likes it or not. Nothing to fear from this adult, or whatever he is. What Cyril gives off is a solitariness like his own, as he looks at his nephew unlike the way other adults look. Is that his idleness, or is he another kind of person, his brown eyes soft and sleepy. Has he slipped away slyly into somewhere different? It could be the nights, he thinks, months and years of nightwork that has made Cyril a little remote, not properly in the daylight world, perhaps not wanting to be. Lean, like all the Callow males, he swims around in a blank darkness and looks out of it, vague through those mild eyes. Younger than his father but really of no age, sunk out of sight from the world. His mother hands him his tea and then teases him. The watching boy knows there is a game going on between them.

"Where's your top set?" she will say, because one of his dentures is always missing. "Sore," he murmurs. "Get it seen to, then, lazy devil," she tells him, but fondly, knowing it is only words: he won't overcome his idleness to do anything he can postpone.

How can this be, a grown man, an adult, whom he sees as a friend? Imaginary it might be, a wordless friendship on his part only, but if his uncle wants an errand doing he asks gently, friend to friend, tells him to keep the change and he is off like a shot. No other uncle leaves his bike propped at the kerb outside the house. There it is, Cyril's steed. All he has is a red scooter, and this rusty machine looks huge, like a five-barred gate. His uncle lets him take it on errands, and he goes wheeling it proudly or scooting along the gutters, one foot on a pedal, steering, squeezing the brakes, ringing the bell. Off to the post office in Ford Street for postal orders, to the newsagent for Craven A or the *Passing Show*. Trying to keep his balance and not fall disgracefully sideways into the road. Quickly he is growing up, but Cyril stays the same eternally youthful uncle. Little by little he creeps into his uncle's world.

Cyril lives half out of sight with his parents in Pinley Gardens at the top of a hill on the edge of town – his brothers and sister have flown away – in a big frame bungalow built by the three sons after the Great War, sheeted with asbestos and a slate roof, on a quarter of an acre of land where he and his brother run wild and hide. When his grandfather comes off duty with his square attache case he marches down his rows of gooseberry bushes as if checking a line of wagons. Or squints out suspiciously through the window at his apples.

"Why don't you count them?" the old lady asks.

"He does," Cyril says from behind his paper.

"Look at the guard," she mocks, as he goes out stubbornly to look.

Chapter 2

Go back. He is no more than four, having his tonsils removed at home. Afterwards he remembers fragments, nightmarish details that quickly fade. In talks with his mother in years to come he reconstructs the scene. Descending the stairs in his pyjamas. In the living room the wall facing the range is wooden, the stairs rising behind this matchboard partition. Near the bottom he stops, peering into the room through the cracks in the boards. Often he does this, pressing his face to the boards, fascinated by the vision of a room seen through a crack. Now he sees the doctor and the anaesthetist by the window, and under the window is the table where they eat meals, now covered in a rubber sheet padded with a blanket underneath.

One man lifts him up on to the table. His mother puts a pillow beneath his head and stands there in silence, intimidated, wringing her hands. A rubber bib is tucked under his chin. The doctor tells him not to be afraid, to think of school, though he is not yet at school, or of playing with his friends. "Think of anything at all," and he thinks of rubber, how he hates the smell, the cold slimy feel of it. He hears a tap dripping in the kitchen, into the white bowl where he washes himself in the mornings. If only it could be such a morning.

A rubber mask comes down over his face. He stares up at the ceiling, rubber under his nose, pressing on his skin, and smells the hateful smell. A voice says, "Breathe very deep." He breathes in, smelling something sweet and sickly mixed with the rubber, tasting it in his mouth. The water dripping in the kitchen is magnified, ping pong, louder and clearer. From far off a voice drones, "Breathe slow and deep," and now the dripping is like the crash of hammer blows. He feels himself slipping, falling into space, clutching to save himself and finding only space. When he wakes he is upstairs in his bed. A few minutes later he is sick, his mother changing the sheet. All he can think of is the falling, the frantic clutching at space, and how he loves lying there under the crisp white sheet, snug and safe with his tonsils out.

Soon the day dawns when it has to happen, leaving his mother's warm side and safe haven, the iron range at its heart always glowing bright. He is taken to All Saints Church of England school at the end of the street and delivered up to Miss Allen. Such tender hands she has, milky white, such a nice calm voice, she is so tall, smiling. His heart fluttering, he is taken outside by the hand. This is the playground, off you go, don't be afraid, don't run too fast, don't fall. He runs round and round like the others. Chases a boy, but not playing tick like them. The boy wears a curious round felt hat and he, the pursuer, only wants to touch it. No way the hunted boy can know there is nothing to fear.

Soon this tiny school is like another home to him. Everything is small-scale, the tiled windowsills, little windows, posies of flowers in jam-jars, the clay pots on saucers. No grim desks, just small tables pushed together, and by their feet the flat tins and boxes the children have brought in, all different, to store pencils and slates. His is a cardboard box labelled Woodbines – still pungent with the smell of tobacco, tiny grains lodged in the corners. He has got it himself from the tobacconist's next door to the *Crown* cinema: "Please can I have an empty box, Mister?"

The boy on his left is Ken Abel, soon to be his hero, his bare knees scratched and scabby, in the same wool jersey and thin tie with horizontal stripes as himself, a cap somewhere for wet days. Everything pervaded by an enveloping sweetness, a tender atmosphere he will miss bitterly when he moves on to the big school. For the time being everything is homely and warms the heart. Unbelievable he thinks later, that he could have gone happily to school, looking forward to it, where no one felt oppressed, or they would never have sung like angels all together, singing "All things bright and beautiful", his heart bursting and innocent, ignorant of the ways of the world, the simple shining faces innocent of fear, singing in unison of "little flowers that open" and "little birds that sing". He is one of these flowers, these birds. How it will make him ache in the desolate years to come, the lost heaven of it. Suffer the little children to come unto Me. Truly he is in heaven every day with Jesus.

And such a homely heaven. Friday afternoons you carry in your own picture books to look at, and always in the afternoons he is encouraged to have a nap, and if he does not want to he pretends. Rests his head on his crossed arms and closes his eyes, and when he wakes up he is still in heaven. A wooden slide comes out on rainy days if it is too wet in the playground. There is dancing round a small Maypole, holding coloured ribbons.

Trying to recapture the joy and bliss later he can only think of the lovely tenderness of those days, when a mere sensation of wonder can make him so happy, so rapt. The moment of bliss he remembers and longs for so intensely later comes one December morning in the Parochial Rooms, a rambling brick building of dusty bare rooms used by the school for concerts. It is a rehearsal for their Christmas concert, and there is a mystery for him in being on the top floor of this echoing building at this special time, smelling the dust, standing on the platform with the paper chains up, hanging over the lights, draping the doorway. He sings *Away in a Manger* with the others, caught up in the close harmony, thrilled by the nearness of Christmas and the marvellous signs of it, the red crêpe pinned along the front edge of the platform, the bare boards creaking under his feet, and he thinks how beautiful are the words "The stars in the bright sky". One of his classmates sings a solo, "Little Old Lady", and he marvels at the boy's fresh clear voice and loves him as he loves the whole simple scene, the grey light hardly creeping into the high room, the time of the day and the adventure of being out of the classroom, above all the sparkling season to come.

One night, safe in his bed, his brother nearby in another narrow bed, he plunges into hell. There is a butcher's shop a few doors along the street, and in two rooms above live a couple with three children. They have to reach their rooms by the back way, down the entry behind his house, but he never sees them. In the yard behind the butcher's is a lean-to corrugated iron shed Peering over the fence he can see the couple's pram, the sides of meat, hung carcasses. Sometimes a sickening smell wafts over. Chunks of fat and gristle lie about in the dirt of the yard. He is fascinated in spite of himself, in spite of his disgust.

He wakes up with a jolt, trembling with fear. His grandfather snores peacefully in his old bedstead in the middle of the room. He can hear battering, splintering sounds, like furniture being thrown and smashed. A woman screams violently, on and on. Doors open, voices shout questions, somebody yelling, "Hey, what's the bloody game?" A voice he thinks he recognises cries, "Fetch the police!" The battering and screaming start up again. He lies shivering in the awful silence that follows. A baby cries wildly, like the voice of his terror. Unable to stop shaking, he strains to listen, hearing raised voices and shocked whispering in the street, under the bedroom window. Pity and horror claw at him until he dozes off. The next day he overhears scraps of talk: the man had come home drunk and begun smashing things and beating his wife.

Playmates. The boy with the curious grey felt hat which has a brim like a girl's has a name which means something to his mother: Roland Harbourne. The father is a tailor. Over the shop in Gosford Street is where they live, and there is the boy's surname above the shop window. When they become friends he is taken up there. He looks round in wonder at this upstairs home, called a flat. "It's a flat," his mother says. "Is it posh in there?" Like his name, she must mean. It is large, warm, luxurious, soft-carpeted: another world. Stocked with expensive toys, anything that Roland, an only child, wants. Roland lolls on the soft floor, heaps of toys and books strewn about carelessly. He only knows that these toys are to be admired and touched, but not played with. Not like with Jack McConnell, his best friend across the entry next door, who shares everything with him.

A square of grass grows in Jack's backyard and in the summer they sit there, cranking away at Jack's toy crane, which is painted red and has a rachet. The sound of the rachet as the cord with its hook unwinds is Jack, it is how he is, his essence, busy and exciting, to be relied on. Jack sits with him in the open shed at the end of his own backyard, playing happily in the dirt, sharing everything. Wonderful

11

it is, side by side, then all of a sudden a catastrophe, they fall out. Jack gathers up his things and goes home, bangs shut his gate.

Deserted, his best friend bursts into tears, his world in ruins. Life can't go on, but it does. The freezing loss and heartbreak are forgotten next day. Jack smiles at him and the sun comes out: all is secure. And one day an extraordinary thing. Jack is alone in his house, his parents out, and he stands behind him as Jack takes a swig from the big jug of milk in the cool secrecy of the pantry, something he would never have dared to do. But his parents don't have a pantry and he stands in this wonder, so dim and still, with its quarry-tiled floor. Jack becomes his hero from this incredible moment.

And there is Ken Abel and one or two others, Eric Adams, sometimes a tight street gang of four or five, off for expeditions along the filthy dribble of the Sherbourne, Coventry's so-called river choked with rubbish and mud, and on dark winter nights the back entries are paths through a trackless jungle. Whoever has a torch is leader: he follows single file with the others, loyal to the death, tested by formidable obstacles like walls he has to climb, holes in fences to crawl through.

A little older and he is the owner of a trolley, a rough plank fitted with pram wheels on their axles, the front wheels swivelling as he tugs at the ropes. Cyril builds it under the stern eye of his father, who makes sure it is safe. Now the shallow gradients of side streets are transformed into hills: on the glacier slopes of pavements he trundles down full of daring, trailing his foot for a brake. And after his father takes him to a race meeting at Brandon Speedway, hoisted on his back to see better, in his nostrils the burnt petrol smell, in his ears the deafening roar and howl of the skidding bikes, he dirt-tracks on his scooter around the corners of back entries. Another boy, Ernest Cooper, is added on to the gang, and on special occasions he is invited in to this strangely different house, eating bread in big crusty chunks toasted on a fancy brass fork at the vertical grill of their range, served with fat knobs of butter on the sizzling gold. He sites with his friend, feet tucked in on the hearthrug, two meek angels out of Dickens on either side of the hearth. Why does it taste ambrosial in Ernest Cooper's home and not in his own?

All through his growing up his grandfather is there, wedged in his grubby armchair with its fetid cushion. His hair thin, but still black like his daughter's. The scurf drops down on his shoulders. He used to comb his grandfather's hair for fun, creating the dead straight parting, but now he no longer does. The old man sits there, a fixture, reading his thrillers, safe in his stone deafness beneath the smouldering gaze of his son-in-law.

One Saturday he and his brother go with him to spend an evening with Derek, the plating shop foreman, a young childless married man in a spanking new house on one of the raw spreading estates along the Birmingham Road. Another bewildering experience, a home totally unlike his, modern, shiny and large, Derek springing about, treating his grandfather with tender deference like a fond son, shouting, "Come on Ted, come and have some tea" into the old man's ear, tugging gently at his arm, sitting them all down, his silent wife smiling and disappearing, and then another wonder, the skittle board out on the table, the swinging ball on a chain and the wooden peg of skittles sent flying once he has mastered it. And never feeling out of place, enveloped in the warmth of Derek's welcome for his grandfather, who sits like a Buddha with a little smile under his straggle of moustache, saying "ah" and "gerrout" if he manages to catch the sense of anything. Ah, the bright sparkling cleanliness of it all in there, new chairs and tables, new bright cushions, and Derek and his subdued wife looking so spruce and sharp, so pleased with their well-ordered life, so prosperous. Oh, the great picture windows letting in floods of light, walls and ceilings slick with fresh paint, the blues and pinks and yellows, and outside the clipped grass and the raked gravel, no sign of a weed.

Going home again is like creeping into a dark hole, like something hollowed out from the street, dark and shrunk, dingy. And suddenly he understands what poor is. Everything worn, shabby, clean because his mother is always endlessly scrubbing and cleaning, but somehow her efforts are in vain, nothing lets in the light, nothing shines except the silver-plated egg cups and cruet that were a wedding present, kept in a cupboard, taken out and cleaned but never used.

Outside at the rear a dairy clanking, a stink of rancid milk in the air. Beyond that, filling the sky, the immense black bulk of the Morris building, thick with windows, covered in iron zigzagging fire-escapes. Upstairs, he and his brother are often awake by the matchboard partition which hides the stairs, listening as their grandfather winds up the big pendulum clock below that belongs to him and then ascends. Once in the bedroom his routine never varies, dragging off his trousers, if it is winter leaving on his long woollen underpants, falling on his knees to mumble a prayer and clambering into his brass bed, watched through the slits of eyes, the worn springs sagging as he rolls around and groans, felled by sleep in a matter of minutes.

After the plating shop job he is for a time a dustman, then a Walls Ice Cream seller. No denying he looks comical in his dustman's armour, a scuffed leather harness over his head and strapped round his waist so that his shoulders will be protected from the brutal-looking heavy bins he has to hoist up. In this carapace the old man is like a blind beetle, but by now his grandson is old enough to feel pity for this short submissive deaf man he always sees as old. He looks away so as not to know him. The ice-cream uniform is sad and funny too but the old man grins under his peaked cap, and the white jacket makes him look weirdly clean, almost a stranger. He squirms on the saddle of his tricycle to reach the pedals and trudges on foot up the hills with his refrigerated box on wheels. Stop Me And Buy One. Standing with his brother at the mouth of the entry when it is time for their grandfather to appear. Slowly and wearily round the corner into view he pedals, the slow grin of recognition dawning at the sight of them, waiting greedily for the free snow-fruits he always dishes out, fumbling with broken fingernails at the thick lid of the box. Cold rises out of it like steam.

He is old enough now to beg pennies from his mother before racing round the corner by the school on some mornings to join the queue of children outside the cake shop, asking for stale cakes and broken biscuits. For tuppence you can get a bagful of buns and rock cakes a day or two old if you are lucky. It is not hunger, but the need to join in, to be like the others, that drives him. And one day the little miracle of being chosen to go with a classmate through the streets in charge of the wicker linen basket full of fresh eggs donated by the school to the charity hospital, a white cloth over the precious cargo, he gripping one handle and his partner the other. Walking very gingerly so as not to stumble, entrusted with this task, feeling happier with every step. He is happier still on the return journey, with absolutely nothing to worry about, just an empty basket he can swing or let drop, even wear like a hat over them both if there is a shower of rain.

How to do justice to your parents, around whom your whole being revolves: the dark sun of your father, the moony mystery of your mother. He is aware of his father's gravity, his mother's meekness. His stalking, tall bones, her small, earth-seeking figure, always retreating back through the door and shutting it, at bay: her instinct to shut out the world. His father comes in, bone-weary, worn down by his struggle to keep the roof over their heads, the food in their mouths. Falls asleep over his paper and his mother watches him anxiously, never relaxing herself, never taking to her bed no matter how ill she feels. No words, but her thin figure is eloquent, her nervous hands fetching and carrying, her brown eyes anticipating the worst, alarmed by the knock on the door, the rent man, the doctor, the child with a pain. It all threatens, strikes fear. What if her protector should fall sick, if a child gets lost? He goes off to school and can feel her eyes on his back anxiously watching, although the school is so close it can be seen at the end of the street. One is conscious of martyrdom.

Yet on the photographs, the cheap blurry snaps taken on summer holidays when they go camping at Barford outside Warwick, there she is set free into another life, the bandanna around her black hair, the white blouse and gypsy skirt, laughing as she must have done as a girl. He sees his mother as a girl emerging from the grind of everyday street living, married drudgery, suddenly free as the air, beautiful in her freedom. The whole area is uncomplicated, effulgent, the village, the road, the bridge, the ford, the baker's shop, the meadows and oaks and chestnuts, willows, the river with its reeds, currents, shallows, pebbles, rapids, mud, minnows. It is an idyll he can only visit and leave, but while he is there he has a different mother. The sunshine becomes her, his father cleans the tin plates, the tent yawns invitingly, the o-p sits in his shirtsleeves on the grass of the field as if mildly surprised to be there. It is a vision of what might be. The simple life! His grandfather squats like a bemused animal and his grandson sits astride a real animal, the farm goat they have made into a pet, his parents on their guard because it will eat anything: wisp of beard and crafty yellow eyes like a farmer. He makes a mascot of it and clings to its curved horns while it stands there, motionless as a donkey in the summer heat, as that creaking peace descends and he walks scuffing his feety in dirty canvas plimsolls, feeling whole and blessed as only a town boy can. Empty flat fields under his feet, and as he walks, at one with insects, birds, particles of dust, fissures in the ground, even gateposts sunk in stillness as if they have been there forever.

His brother lolls in the sun. Nearby is the slow river, a great lure for his father who likes to fish. All wrapped around in a oneness that is bound to end. In years to come the comical goat stories will be told and retold. How it tried to eat the guy-ropes. His mother crossing the farmyard at twilight, the suddenly devilish goat prancing out from behind a barn with its head lowered, so that she screams and runs: his father fishing on the river bank, looking up to find himself trapped by a goat made crazy by twilight. Perhaps not such an ordeal for a man who has survived the carnage of war, joining under-age in 1914 and off to France before his mother can stop him, serving in one of the first tanks and coming home unscathed but as if sworn to silence, the awful slaughter locked within him. Over the living room door a weird trophy hung on a nail, his shrapnel mask, shaped leather with slits to see through, a fringe of fine chainmail hanging below. Nothing to do but go to and fro under it and ask no questions. His father says nothing. He is discouraged from having toy guns, and so is his brother, but Buffalo Bill and Tom Mix on the screen seduce him. He wears a toy silver revolver in a holster when his father is out of the house.

Chapter 3

Barford lives in him as a summer idyll, an undying story he retells in his heart, flat pastures and a river enveloped in country smells, with its own time, its farmer remembered for his one phrase, "Windy betimes". Pinley Gardens is idyllic but not a dream, not a holiday place, because by some extraordinary accident he magically belongs there. And the extraordinary accident is his grandmother.

"Bless him, then," she cries, bent over some task in the lean-to kitchen, as she catches sight of him peering in at her through the open door. "Why, hello, my love! Well I never, well I never! Have you come to see poor old Granny? Come here, come to me, ducky!"

Her tender smile melts his heart, a smile of such sweetness that it strikes root in his memory, a secret root of joy in his childhood, blossoming forth in dark moments, a tender foliage. Her soft cries of delight, her vigorous laughter, ring in his ears again.

Seeing him, all the burden of her hard life seems to fall away. Her crippled, swollen hands flutter like birds with excitement as she gathers him in her arms and presses him to her strongly, with such a fierce and tender joy. It is as if the young give her such delight that she becomes young again herself, transformed by her own happiness. Her back remains stooped, her thin hair snowy white, but she no longer seems old. "Want to see the banties with your Granny?" she cries, snatching up his hand, and takes him down the path towards the shed with the bucket lavatory and its two seats, past the apple trees against the hedge and the pit filled to the brim with stagnant water, covered in slimy boards, that has two fat frogs always in residence. Inside a wooden frame stretched with wire netting are the five pretty Bantam hens, which he is allowed to feed. He has heard about the night-soil men who call after midnight once a fortnight to empty the contents of the bucket lavatory into the cart no one ever sees.

Long after his grandparents have died he can remember, almost smell the odour of paraffin in the bungalow, called *Tavistock* because his grandmother was once in service in Plymouth. No electricity, smoky paraffin lamps and Valor stoves for heating. He loves arriving to push open the gate and enter beneath what he calls the snowball tree, with its mass of white fluffy blossoms. Along the back of *Tavistock* runs a high verandah of slatted wood overlooking the Humber and Austin factories down below, for him to stand gazing over the spread of Coventry, a sea captain before the broken water of roofs.

Pinley Gardens is a huddle of shacks in a hollow, dirt roads between that are no more than wide bumpy tracks full of pot-holes and loose shale, a slum community of factory workers, railwaymen like his grandfather, working men with enterprise and no money who'd managed to claim a parcel of land and build shacks, some of them now squalid. He walks through this colony on his way to and from *Tavistock*, which was once the first, its plot of land the biggest, and the area's strangeness fascinates him, though he hears it condemned as a shanty town by his parents. Cyril always cracks the joke about the woman in one of the shacks who empties her chamber pot out of the window with a grand gesture, imitating her for their amusement.

Patrolling his verandah he is in heaven, sometimes the captain of a ship, sometimes on a Mexican ranch, and the aluminium ventilators on the squat roofs of workshops become the peaks of glittering mountains. Kneeling down to peer through the slats he can see water glinting underneath in the storage tank, and farther back a big heap of coal ready for the winter, and perhaps the glowing green eyes of a cat that has sought the shade.

It is the best place on earth, and he knows it. Now and then he is allowed to stay the night, alone or with his brother, once for a whole fortnight during his school holidays in August. He loves the smell of raspberry bushes when he hides among them, the rhubarb leaves like elephant's ears, limp in the heat. The spaniel bitch, Judy, races to meet him, an amazingly gentle creature, following him everywhere like a slave, waiting outside his bedroom door for him to get up. The odour of paraffin would reach him, and gradually the delicious breakfast smells. "God bless you, you're awake!" cries his grandmother, bending over to touch his face. "Up you get then, I've laid the table. Are you hungry, my love?"

How she loves him to be ravenous. Afterwards, lying on the sunken lawn that they use occasionally for badminton, he experiences the sensation of being on a great hairy flag which flaps under his back if he closes his eyes tight. Judy comes and licks devotedly at the roots of his hair. Hour after hour he absorbs the sun on these hot August days, until he staggers on his legs like a bee. Lying there half drunk with heat he brings into his mind the large Victorian print in the dark corridor outside his bedroom, depicting the interior of one of the great London stations. He imagines walking under the vast, arched cavern, smoke-filled, swarming with tiny figures, thrilling himself with the touch of fear.

Tavistock, in open country when it was built, is to him country still. Pinley Gardens is rural, a green place of fruit bushes and new-laid eggs, water pumped up laboriously in the kitchen from a well, and at night the world outside pitch-black. Vecqueray Street seems a hundred miles away. Cyril, spoiled by his old mother, has commandeered the front room for his own use as the one remaining son. A full-sized billiard table swallows half the space, and round the piano once a month two workmates from the factory help him murder the classics: violin, piano and cello, a grave chamber trio sawing away deadly serious and concentrated, then at the end hoots of triumph as they get there together. And to that sanctuary of a room he marches up on Sunday mornings for violin lessons, sometimes waiting for his uncle to finish his breakfast. Cyril has bought him his violin, a cheap one. He learns to read music after a fashion, taking sheet music home to astonish his mother with "Twinkle twinkle little star". Terrible squeaking mistakes over and over, until she begs, "Can you stop now, please?" He takes more readily to the rules of billiards.

His first memories are thronged with callers, and though their numbers diminish they still appear. He remembers callers who knocked on the back door and stood begging, or audaciously asked, callers for the rent (kept in a tea caddy with the rent book on the mantelpiece), doctors who had the front door left ajar for them, callers who sang out a greeting and came in, who were expected. Callers who were part of the life of the street were the milkman, the bread man, the coal man, and at Eastertime the man shouting hoarsely that he had hot-cross buns for two a penny or four a penny. Most numerous were the tramps, calling often, stringy bristle-faced men knocking for cans of water and some bread, the boldest wanting an old shirt or a pair of trousers. Up on the entry wall outside they put a chalk mark to indicate that this was a good place, the mark high up, out of reach and dry.

Hawkers and gypsies were always pushy, insinuating, hard to turn away. Most dramatic was the rag-and-bone man when he stuck his fierce shaggy head over the weatherboard fence and bawled his singsong. He carried a greenish bugle. Out in the street he stopped and blew three rasping notes towards the blind windows.

Then there were one or two regular Sunday morning callers. One man he knew as Uncle George was not really an uncle but an old friend of the family. He plodded in blandly like a top-heavy bear, unbuttoning his thick brown overcoat as he advanced, squashing into the small warm room with his huge body and strong smell. He smelled of tobacco and public houses. It was George's custom to walk with his dog across the common, and as he turned to come back the pubs would be opening. He called at the *Spread Eagle*, stayed for half an hour and then made for Vecqueray Street.

His old black dog had an odour as heavy as its master. Waddling down the entry from the street it always paused to cock its leg stiffly with great deliberation and soak the bottom of the wall.

Once wedged into the small room, George rested the hook of his walking stick on the table edge and lowered himself into a chair, a slow, anxious operation. He sighed and breathed hard and cleared his throat emphatically, pinning his cap to his knees with stumpy, hairy fingers. His broad neck above his collar at the back was dry, full of cracks and the dark wrinkles of age, weather and dirt. Red patches showed on his enormous loose cheeks. The dog curled itself out of sight under the chair, between feet and trouser-legs as rooted as trees. Burying its grey muzzle it uttered little sounds of resignation.

Sitting there helpless, gazing at the range fire stifled by ashes, George would start to perspire. He pulled out a handkerchief the size of a small flag and mopped painfully at his face.

George's voice had captivated him when he first heard it. Whenever he called it was the same incredible throaty gasp, no louder than a whisper. His mother would poke the fire, and George stirred. He was waiting to be offered a cup of tea.

Another Sunday visitor was Tommy Timms. Sometimes they would go for months without seeing him, and then he would drop in unexpectedly. His mother knew Tommy through the church. He was a bricklayer who had found religion rather late in life. Stiff in his serge suit and a white muffler, he was small, erect, a scrupulously clean man with huge shiny black boots. He had liquid, fervent eyes. Because Tommy was regarded as a bit simple his mother was especially kind to him. When he stretched you could hear the noise of his cracking bones. She was always dismayed when she caught sight of him approaching through the kitchen window because he had no idea of time.

He came in chattering breezily and shaking hands. He was exceedingly formal. "What a surprise, ah what a stranger, well well," he chirped, referring to himself. He bubbled and frothed, waiting on the threshold as always to be invited in.

He was fresh from church, a large bible gripped in his clean fist. "Keeping fit, are you?" they asked him, getting him seated. It was necessary to offer him a chair or he would stand for ever, even though he had been coming for years.

"Fine, yes, fine. Can't grumble."

They asked after his mother.

"She's fine, fine. Wonderful, really." He had lived with her all his life. She had been a widow for twenty years. In her eighties, she suffered from cataracts and arthritis.

"Is she getting about at all?"

"Oh, now and again, you know – now and again."

"And you're keeping busy?" This was a reference to his being recently retired.

"Me? Busy? Oh yes, can't complain, can't grumble."

He sat and sat, smiling broadly and shining, his black hair a block, hands and face lit red, sitting bolt upright like a god. Happiness poured from him.

"Poor Tommy, he's had a terrible life of it," his mother would say afterwards and he puzzled over what she might mean. Was he ridiculed, hunted, chased by boys down the street?

Conversations were invariably a trial. Tommy accompanied whoever was speaking in a series of rapid repetitions, following point by point, skipping after their words and almost stuttering with haste, as if he had been running or was madly excited. He leaned forward from his chair in his anxiety to agree, twisting his red sinewy workman's hands together. He had a large bony nose and prominent fleshy ears. His head looked particularly hard with bones. "Ah yes, dear me – yes, oh yes, good gracious me, yes ... well I'm blessed," he would cry.

If he told a tale of his own or had some news it was quite lifeless, like something unwinding. He droned away, nasal and high-pitched, and no one ever saw the point. There were no climaxes, nothing but flat uniformity. His contentment was terribly monotonous.

Somehow after a while his very voice seemed a trial. When at last he looked at his watch, nodded, hopped off the chair and stood up, flexing his short legs and saying over and over that he would have to go, the very atmosphere approved of him.

The older he grows, the more he likes to be told about himself as a small child behaving badly in ways that are beyond the reach of his memory, that he cannot retrieve for himself. For instance, in an upstairs flat in Warwick where his newly married parents are living he screams "blue murder" when the coalman climbs the stairs and comes in carrying a sack, his face a mask of coal dust. The whole building is alive with rats, he is told later. At another address, he is taken in his pushchair to a railway bridge to see the trains, and when his mother stops to chat he shouts, "Stop talking!" His mother recounts this to others: it amuses her to think of him as a little tyrant. He feels like a monster, yet he likes to hear it.

22

Chapter 4

His father takes any job he can get: it's the Depression. Clerk at the Labour Exchange, on the counter, in daily contact with unemployed, desperate men; at the Humber factory; a machine operator in a bakelite factory. He is even reduced to canvassing door to door for the *Daily Express*, though he votes Labour and speaks of the paper with contempt. Then his luck changes: his army comrade, Jack Higgins, starts up a car delivery and hire business with his brothers in a dilapidated building in Paradise Street, an alley at the top of Gulson Hill. Jack a raw-boned giant, hulking shoulders and craggy jaw like a boxer, product of a hard school. A sepia photo at home shows his father in khaki uniform, soft cap, rimless glasses, squatting behind a machine gun with Jack Higgins standing beside him, hand on his shoulder: a cordial, phlegmatic man, pallid face curiously expressionless.

When he takes his father his lunch one Saturday he finds him in an office like a glass box, raised on a concrete platform. Called a manager, his father bends to his task over a mess of paper, hemmed in by overripe files, spikes loaded with invoices, bulldog clips hanging on nails hammered into the framework. Pale, preoccupied, with his little black moustache and serious-looking glasses, he holds out his hand without lifting his head. At night he comes in wistful and responsible, on his clothes the unmistakable odour of petrol his son has smelled hanging heavily in the air of the cavernous, oily garage.

And one day something momentous – they all go on a visit to Jack's grand new house, a detached house in grounds, built to his own design on the edge of Memorial Park. His father, proud to be invited and excited at the prospect, is too naive to see how his mother is thrown into a crisis. "You're the one who wants to go, poking in your nose," she accuses, then relents, wailing plaintively, "What can I wear?"

"Don't be daft," his father laughs. "It's not royalty, it's Jack Higgins."

"And his wife," moans his mother.

He and his brother are dressed up and inspected, and they set off, his mother crucified in advance with embarrassment. Identified with her, angry at his father's evident obtuseness, he is the speechless witness. His father leads the way up to the large oak door with its lit porch. He follows sheepishly with his mother and brother, understanding the reason for it all: they are there to admire. "Don't stare, it's rude," his mother hisses in a final warning as they enter the blaze of electricity, bright as a department store after their dismal gas mantles. Jack's dressy wife bustling up to fuss and be a guide, over the parquet floors, fitted carpets, bathrooms, central heating, into a room called a lounge that goes off into the distance, an immense heated space. Unable to bear his mother's discomfort he studies Jack Higgins the self-made man, generous with his hospitality, nothing boastful or brash, but underneath the hard streak his father lacks, the astute touch that gives him the edge over his less successful rough brothers who drive the car deliveries. The roughneck subtly transformed, changed by his wealth and power.

He is fully aware by now of how different they all are, his three aunts and four uncles. There is Cyril with his soft wary eyes, his soft limbs, at ease and lazy in the bosom of his family. There is his gentle, rather remote smile. He overhears his father's irritation with Cyril for always taking the easy option. His years on the nightshift at the Standard, well-paid but unchanging, would be intolerable to some men, but for him it means either that or stirring himself to make a change. His intelligence must lie dormant, otherwise it would have forced him from his job, even from the cosy nest of Pinley Gardens, in a new direction. Imagine the upheaval in him if a woman had laid claim to him: after all he would attract the kind of woman drawn to his childishness, the way his narrow shoulders droop, the way he seems to invite mothering. And his gentleness is attractive, and fun lurks behind those soft, unassertive eyes. One day, years after his parents have died and he is forced to fend for himself, he settles in the easy squalor of a terraced house in a side street with an overgrown garden. The woman who comes to clean and shop for him adds him on to her ménage in time and he becomes a fixture there, going on holidays with her and her docile, warehouseman husband. Cyril provides a caravan, takes them places in his capacious Vanguard. Again the line of least resistance, where he is comfortable, where nothing disturbs him because nothing really changes: and there are no demands.

No wonder Cyril infuriates his father, whom he deflects by refusing to take offence, even when Hubert's sardonic comments border on the offensive: the man who has been through a war, subjected to army discipline, goaded by the youngest brother with his unruffled life. Cyril smiles across at his mother, amused by her harmless scolding. "You're always late, you're hopeless," she cries, and he blinks sleepily and smiles. Always she is ready to indulge him.

"Hallo, May," comes his creastfallen greeting, his little-boy, implicit apology on his bleary-eyed, good-looking face.

"I suppose you still want a cup of tea. Aren't you late for work?"

He rubs his head, as if trying to wake up, to register the question. His nephew knows it is a game. "Nah." His mother shaking her head in mock disgust, secretly glad to see him, going off to fill up the kettle.

He likes best the Saturday night suppers now and then, when Cyril has been liberated from his factory and drops in, always on the off-chance, letting no one know in advance. "Can't be bothered, can he," his father mutters, to no avail. Cyril pays as a matter of course: his eager nephew is dispatched to Conolly's for the fish and chips, made hungry by the smell of frying, the dry shake of the salt, the squirt of vinegar in liberal splashes, sheets of newspaper ripped up for parcelling, steam billowing into the street from the open door, winter and summer. Out into the night with his mother's shopping bag, and at home on the laid kitchen table his mother has the plates warmed and ready, the sliced tomatoes, a heap of buttered bread in fat white slices, the tea made. Jumps up for the pickled onions, hovers to fetch this and that. "Sit down, woman," his father says, but when does she ever settle in one place for more than a minute? She hovers, worries, selfless as a servant but somehow in charge of everything. She makes everything go.

He has a sense of himself in relation to his brother; initiating games because his brother is four years behind, the baby with golden, slowly darkening curls who is no problem, unlike him with his temper tantrums, his sudden stomach aches, attacks of constipation: not a naughty boy but a worry. His brother with his chubby cheeks, bright hair and amenable nature will soon develop a stubborn streak and find ways of resisting his pushy need to be in charge, to assert his superior strength. For the time being the angelic brother submits, as he organises games using upturned chairs on the floor for a bus, he the conductor and his kid brother the passenger. He had a conductor's outfit for Christmas, a cap with a cardboard peak, a bunch of tickets, a tinny punch that rings a bell when you punch a fare. Already there are spasms of protest. "Ask for a ticket, go on." "Don't want to." "Where are you going?" "Don't know." "Say Broadgate – go on, say it." "No." He is half ashamed of his bullying will, but he is older, stronger. Using picture books opened as tunnels for the clockwork train to run through. On summer evenings out in the dusty park to play cricket, finding bricks to stand up as wickets, his brother bowling underarm, not wanting to go on into the twilight. "Can we go home now?" "Get me out first." "No, now." The melancholy lengthening of shadows on the withered grass, the park deserted, half liking the sad feeling, the sound of rooks gathering.

The expedition one summer day with his brother to a field on the city boundary where they had once picnicked as a family is a foretaste of things to come, where one is undermined by demons of doubt inside oneself. He takes a small ridge tent for them both to lie down in if the sun is too hot, and there are sandwiches and fat bottles of pop and a rolled groundsheet in the two haversacks slung on their backs. He walks off stoutly to catch the bus, the grave, responsible leader, their mother waving on the doorstep. He has the heaviest load, being the elder. "Watch the traffic, won't you? Look after your brother."

Dwindling pathetically she waves them out of sight, and he is undermined at the outset by her nervous fear, trying not to look back until they turn the corner. Goodbye! Why does it have to be such a sorrowful event – they will be away for a matter of hours. Tramping down to the bus station at Pool Meadow for a 28 to the terminus, to

Baginton not far from the aerodrome. He knows the field, its exact location: cross-examined by his mother he has said yes, he knows, get off at the terminus, go over the little hump-backed bridge and there it is, the field where they have all been. How could there be danger? Nevertheless his mother is riddled with doubts, his father merely shrugging with the comment that it is part of growing up, to do things on your own.

There it is, but not as he remembers it. Not welcoming at all. Foliage has run riot and exhausted itself, huge dusty nettles in the ditches, dock leaves, the summer bolted and gone to seed, hanging there as if in despair. He has a bad feeling which he keeps to himself. He wonders if this is somehow wrong, picking his way through the nettle beds gingerly, and then he sees the dried-up stream choked with big jagged stones, the baked mud punctured with hoof-holes where cattle have trampled down the low bank for a watering place. Yes, this is the spot alright, only now it is subtly changed. No parents, no protection, now everything bristles, looks hostile. His brother stumbles on the rough hummocks, twists his foot in a rut and whimpers.

The very silence is frightening, and the air of desertion. Suddenly he hates it, the field is ugly in a malignant, menacing sort of way. He struggles against a desire to run off home. Without speaking he unpacks the tent and starts to erect it, the pegs more like meat skewers, to be shoved into the ground with the heel of your hand. They hurt: the ground is iron-hard. One after the other the skewers bend. He feels they are unwanted by the field, the ground, by everything.

Biting his lip he goes searching for a softer spot, the darkness rising inside him, his brother staying put, squatting in the wilderness like the very personification of defeat. Overhead the sky clouds over and lowers like a lid, all without a breeze, in absolute silence. He asks his brother what is the matter and gets the answer, "Nothing."

Pitching camp again, he spreads the groundsheet as if they are really staying but he knows it is pretence. Somehow he has to bluff it out a little longer. He sites nervously with his brother in the tent mouth, flaps rolled back and fastened with tapes; inside, behind them, that snug womb-like look a small tent has, the yellow filtered light on the grey groundsheet. It looks inviting but he has lost faith in it. He sits there hugging his knees, munching the soggy tomato sandwiches and guzzling the fizzy strawberry pop, glancing round uneasily as if expecting to be eaten alive by something. He can't wait to get away. The weather is his excuse; his brother raises no objection. He senses that his brother is scared too, though he might have caught the feeling of apprehension from him. Where has *he* caught it from? He doesn't wait to ask, it is such a relief going.

If it is an attack of homesickness out of nowhere, it is nothing like the desolate feeling of loss he experiences when he goes off alone on a camp with the scouts for a week, his first time away from home. Kingswear in Devon, narrow lanes with steep leafy banks dropping down to the ferry, Dartmouth opposite with its quays and hotels – a lush creamy landscape opening and folding its hills, great ferny slopes giving off waves of fragrance, and suddenly on the crest of an amazing new world, the sky a stroke of surprise, the sea far below shivering its skin; and the huge light. The washed sea air inside his shirt, up his legs. To be tipped off the lorry with all the tents and equipment into such a world, lying at night in the lofty bell tent with the others, feet to the pole, and all he does is ache for the nondescript street where his mother lives, nothing else, blind and deaf to everything else, counting the hours and days, his whole being tuned to one far-off point of departure. He finds he is in a labour camp, up at six digging latrines, detailed to help with breakfasts, with washing up, great heaps of potatoes to be peeled, ordered on cross-country races while the senior scouts and rovers loaf on the grass as supervisors, sunburnt and handsome giants with big thighs and hairy forearms. All week they lord it over him and his Peewit patrol, joking among themselves, clearly conscious of being an elite. He is too young and too intimidated to question anything. At night he buys chocolate and slabs of toffee from the tuck shop and lies in his sleeping bag chewing until he is nearly sick, not once ceasing to long desperately for home, every waking second, in all the fibres of his body.

Chapter 5

Uncle Bill is the uncle with protruding teeth, and a mop of stiff curly fair hair that enhances some essential springiness about him. The middle one of the three brothers, with his father the eldest, the wide splitting grin is full of cheek. Somehow the prominent teeth make him positive, personal, almost handsome.

He likes Uncle Bill without knowing why. Registers the charm of his personality, his quick vivacious grin, his fizz. It bounces fizzing out of his eyes, he comes in on a wave of exuberance and stands with hands on his hips. In large gauntlets, legs spread like a warrior, asking how we are. Addressing no one in particular.

Always his mother is incensed by him, saying "What a cheek he's got," the moment he shoots off. "What's he after now?" His father might say, "He wanted to borrow my brace and bit."

"Did you lend it him?"

"Why not?"

"What did I tell you?"

"What?"

"He's after what he can get. He only comes when he wants something."

"Don't be daft."

"You're too soft to see it."

The last thing he would call his father is soft. His mother means naive, gullible. What his father likes about Bill is his force, his movement, the absence of which he so deplores in Cyril. For himself, he likes it when his uncle asks him with a broad toothy grin how it is with him. "How's life, kid?" Blushing he says he is all right, thank you.

"That's the stuff to give 'em."

And something that sticks in his mind for years afterwards: "Whenever I see your lad he's got a blue shirt on. Blue as a bluebottle." Ignoring this, his mother asks after Bill's wife: "How's Ivy?"

He lounges against the wall. "Fine, the last time I saw her," he says, knowing this will enrage his mother, and it does. Her mouth a tight line. Going, he leaves door and gate open behind him, to his mother's disgust. "Your Bill all over. All he thinks about is Number One." To which his father doesn't respond.

No darkness yet in his world, except the shadows cast by money worries and a mother always struggling with her dread of a life hedged about with ogres – the teachers from her girlhood, now doctors, officials of all kinds, nearly all men, and by the threat of disease. Worst of all, the fear of being reduced to abject poverty and ending in the workhouse, still an institution as bleak as Dickens with its iron gates open like jaws at the top of Gulson Hill. About to close for good but its horrors enshrined in legend, men and women cruelly segregated in old age, stripped of rights. On the way up to the Co-op, holding his mother's hand, he peers in at hobbling figures bent over in the grim cobbled yard, chopping firewood. How the chill of it must pierce her heart, and just as surely, holding her hand, the chill is transferred without words to him.

Bill laughs at her fears, not callously but from the overflow of his vigorous presence. No time for imaginary threats; he has a living to make, odd jobs, anything. In a thick tweed overcoat with a belt, the collar a bit yellowish, he strides about in the thick of life, not stopping to ask questions. Boisterous is how his nephew sees him, with his contradictory lean body, imagining him somehow untamed, and where he lives with his tall wife Ivy and two infants out at Corley Moor suits his view of him. Thinking of it as a wild, crude, country region, though in fact only five miles from the city, the moor just a strip of heath covered in brambles and bracken. Like a foreign land to him. He says there a time or two with his brother in a raw new house that is bare and cold, on a barren plot that has chickens and at the far end by the broken fence looking out on blank fields some pigs, rooting around inside a dirty bell tent, ripping up the ground with their broad snouts. He remembers candle ends, cabbage stalks, torn newspaper, the casual squalor of it, as foreign to him as the raw houses in the middle of nowhere, like town houses that have lost their street.

There is a shop called The Stores at the bottom of a long hill. The bell tinkles, the floor is bare planks, all the contents look fly-blown, nobody comes to serve for a long time and a baby wails in the back. Nearby a pub with peeling paint, the *Rising Sun*.

He doesn't like it there, then is revived and feels cheerful when Bill drives up in his green three-wheeler van from delivering butter and eggs. He hopes to ride in the van, which is without doors and instead of a steering wheel has the handlebars and controls of a motorbike. He gets his wish, loving the hectic way his uncle leaps out like a spring at each call, squeezing the black rubber bulb of his horn to signal his arrival. He loves the recklessness of his driving, the occasional curse, the careless gust of his life.

In the cheerless house his Aunt Ivy stands silent, like an Indian squaw must be, he imagines, always in the kitchen, willing to accept Bill as he is; a tall grave figure with large capable hands, a slow smile and no words at all. He likes it when Bill winks at him suddenly, a man ready to turn his hand to anything, who will teach himself upholstery, start a firm with his wife's brothers, and will soon involve himself in the ferment of Labour politics, impatient for change, to make something happen. At the front of the house is a flower bed with nothing in it, a patch of grass and a stone fence, somehow forlorn and pointless since there is nothing to keep out, and beyond it just the empty lane and a thorn hedge and then nothing again. Beyond, the scrubland of the heath, which he thinks of as huge because there are no hedges, just the clouds and kestrels: a dour solitude called the Moor.

Everything speaks of a temporary life. Everything to do with Bill has running through it his fluid nature, his readiness to be flexible, prominent buck teeth breaking out in laughter which is often derisive as he follows his instinct to go along with the natural flow, the humour of life. Bouncing out of his van he comes crunching over the gravel and weeds, and the sight of his impatience is invigorating. His nephew knows he is hardly noticed, otherwise Bill would be an equal favourite like Cyril, whose insouciance enables him to have time for him. Cyril will never master anything; he is stuck in his dreamy adolescence, at ease in his mother's love. Not only is he spoiled but he spoils himself, indulges his tastes, follows his own inclinations, lets himself off. When the war comes it is Bill who takes on full-time rescue work in the rubble of central Coventry as the bombs and incendiaries rain down, his father who joins the ARP, gets bombed and injured. Cyril carries on at the Standard, puts a caravan in a field at Lillington for his old mother and father, goes on in his own sweet way. You feel that he hardly notices the war.

Bill moves into Coventry, and the boy is shocked one evening, on an errand for his mother, to find his uncle in the living room, stretched out full length on the sofa, hands behind his head, wide awake. His aunt is in the kitchen as always. He is astonished and impressed by the sight of Bill looking so utterly relaxed in his own home: there is something oriental about it.

Both uncles are a world away from Fred, the husband of his mother's sister Florrie. They live in Leamington, a sedate town in these days, ten miles to the south and west of Coventry. Strange how it divides in half, above the river and the Pump Rooms with its spa water the well-to-do Georgian houses and mansions, and at the bottom, the other side of the river, the slummy, half industrial grimy streets of cramped terraces, the iron railway bridge over the road, the station, garages, warehouses, small factory premises, junk shops. Florrie and Fred live in a top-floor flat in Clarendon Square, a block of Georgian houses set back from the road. The address says it all: they are in a different universe entirely. Florrie has gone up, got on. A year and a half younger than his mother, fretful and rapid, her demeanour proclaims a difference that fails to obscure what they have in common: the o-p, their slum childhood, a mother dying of throat cancer in her fifties before he was old enough to remember her – in the photos a gaunt, fine-boned, gentle-looking woman. In Florrie is hidden an ingrained knowledge of life once lived at the bottom, surfacing in his mother as a wary, sad smile and a timidity, the cautious smile of the poor anywhere.

And meeting on visits his mother is almost apologetically laughing, her sister ironically aware of their so different circumstances now, her very accent more proper. Not stand-offish, that would have been intolerable, more an acceptance of their very different levels of daily existence. She has no qualms about her elevation, though he does not yet understand the price she has had to pay. The third floor flat, the gracious proportions of the windows, even the shabby stucco of the Georgian building with its patches peeling and cracked, are all symbolic of her change of fortune. So they arrive on visits as the poor relations from Coventry, usually in the afternoon on a weekday and so without the shameful o-p and without his father. Crowding in as excited children to see Aunt Florrie and her daughter Sheila and be made conscious of the gulf, the insuperable difference, feeling oddly privileged and proud. And after all tenuously connected.

Arrives wonderingly, wide-eyed on his first visit, up the rather bleak and cold common staircase used by the other tenants with its institutional green, then entering his aunt's inner sanctum, the dark dog-leg corridor opening yards later on to a landing of space and airiness, high windows full of views, the private gardens down below, across the road, railed around and gated, for which you needed a key, with its dense shrubbery and gravel paths. Again he is in the lounge, that word, where he sits among the splendour of new thirties furniture, gold gleaming wood and clean lines, ceilings out of reach, and is given tea. Afternoon tea belongs to this other world. Florrie chattering as if nothing has really changed, as if this represents her as she truly is, a sparky woman living off her nerves, her laugh shooting up high, alarming him with its touch of hysteria, chattering away for dear life; his mother subdued, responding warmly, laughing in sympathy. Impossible for him to know what she feels, but certainly not envy, he is sure of that. For all its comfort and affluence she would be unhappy living somewhere like this – it is not homely enough. But he has eyes only for an object he had never seen before, a revolving bookcase. Such a symbol of luxury. People with books, with time to read books, a special place for books! He has yet to learn that it is important to give an impression of culture, that things are not what they seem.

Sheila, his cousin, about his age, is on her best behaviour, dolled up for their arrival in a crisply ironed dress, impatient to show off her own part of this kingdom, where she alone reigns. "Can I show them my new wallpaper?" "Not now, darling, there's plenty of time, we're having tea." Sulkily she subsides: bobbed shiny hair, pretty really in a snub-nosed, chubby way. He goes in to inspect her room with its neat, tightly encased bed, looking as if no one ever slept there, the bright patterned quilt and the wallpaper smothered in pink roses.

Another time, when she is more insufferably spoilt than usual, he thinks what a joy it would be to hold her down on the immaculate bed until she kicked and screamed, outraged, her room's sanctity violated.

Yet even with Sheila telling them impudently how special she is, how pampered, he enjoys going there, and likes it too on the double-decker bus returning home, up on the top deck on the front bench seat against the juddering window, he and his brother pretending to steer the giant lumbering bulk of the vehicle round the bends and corners, wrestling with an imaginary steering wheel.

Of course with Fred Jones there it is all different, the atmosphere edgily unnatural, Florrie jumpier than ever, her unnerving laugh shrieking upwards as he becomes more risqué, tongue poking out lewdly from his lipless slit of a mouth. Somehow the presence of company seems to goad Fred to do his utmost to shock. He is fascinated by his uncle's top lip, it looks so sore and bright red in a washed-out white face. Then he sees why. It is his habit of sucking it. At the head of the table if they are having a meal he sits slithery on his bony bottom, itching about, pasty-faced and sucking, his hair slicked back. He has a habit of rubbing his hands dryly, almost frenziedly together between his knees after telling an off-colour joke, tucking in his chin and snickering. Though the boy has no understanding of what is meant, he sees that Fred is under some compulsion to perform, to shock, and he feels shame, sensing that what spills from his commercial traveller's mind is suggestive. He is ashamed for his mother, ashamed even for Florrie having to listen in cold silence between her blurting high-strung laughs that seem on the verge of snapping, as she endures yet again the nasty wit of her Freddie. He is a representative for Lockheed Hydraulic Brakes, on the road for days at a time in the firm's car, a big ostentatious Wolseley that Fred allows him to sit in one day, taking in his suit, a subtle shade of brown, his white cuffs, his suave kid gloves, his thin smirk, eyes flickering sideways in his pallid hairless face, the sumptuous walnut dashboard before him that he would like to touch. None of the humorous careless attitude to life of Bill about Fred, none of the secret, shy inwardness of Cyril with his instinct for slipping through life unobserved. Fred stands for the world at its cheapest, his pale fish eyes calculating the price of everything.

He is miserably conscious of his mother's nervous fear of life, not wanting to be, pitying her almost angrily, not realising that he is prone to the same debilitating weakness. When he is, he wants to protest, to accuse his mother of infecting him. He tries to harden himself against this tendency in her to grieve for the weak and helpless, the unfortunate ones, exasperated like his father by her timid, sorrowful nature. But under the shrinking timidity she is strong, determined, emotionally deep. He has no access to his father's feelings since his father is of a generation which is not demonstrative, whereas he shares times of intimacy with his mother because of a closeness he cannot deny. He is like her. She sees into him. Sometimes she seems to be him. It is uncanny. And under her taut nerves lies her indomitable will.

His mother's simple religious faith, and her attendance three times a day on Sundays as a girl at Christ Church, the smallest of Coventry's three spires, encourages her identification with those who have nothing, who never fail to pierce her heart. In the memoir she writes in old age she will remember going into the slums and courts with a portable harmonium provided by the church, to sing hymns and carols to those even worse off than herself, accompanied by her sister. His father doesn't share her faith, and although he doesn't oppose it either, after her marriage her church attendance ceases. His father's sympathy with the dispossessed expresses itself as a desire to see justice done, a working-class belief in socialism as simple as his mother's religion. When he goes to Sunday School at the baptist chapel in Gosford Street he does so as much to oppose his father as to please his mother. But also because he feels uneasily that he exploits her love shamelessly, takes all and gives nothing in return. This is to misunderstand the nature of her love, which in its essence is sacrificial, asking only to serve. The secret of happiness for her is bound up in giving.

He can recall utterly contented mother-and-son times before he is eleven, all the happier because his mother is carefree, wandering through the market with her on school holidays when they share little jokes, say a woman bearing down on them placidly with a vast shaking bosom, and he whispers from the side of his mouth to shock and amuse her, "Jelly on a plate!" And she blushes like a girl. The man on the stall selling bed linen, plaid tablecloths, thick yellowish working men's vests and long johns like his grandfather's, singing out loud and gutteral whenever the searching women delve too freely, "Nah then, ladies, if you don't want the goods don't maul 'em!" He mimics this war cry when they are home, always pleased when she laughs. "Don't maul 'em, don't maul 'em!" he cries suddenly, to surprise her, to make her jump.

On these market forays he makes a beeline for the magazine and comics counter, his mother fumbling with a pile of comics she has brought from home to trade in – *Hotspurs* and *Skippers* and *Rovers*, never the *Magnet* or *Gem* or *Boy's Own*, turning over the secondhand, dog-eared copies glowing with unread adventures to make sure he hasn't read them already. Follows the ritual of the man calculating what he is owed, his mother paying carefully from the black purse she grips like a lifeline, rearranging her shopping bag to provide room for the spoils. Always the same thing said: "There, that'll keep you out of mischief for an hour or two," and they begin the journey home, arms linked. Passing near the fish counter she says, "Do you fancy some smoked haddock for tea – would you like that?" and he answers ungraciously, "Don't mind." Or fussily, because when he gets the chance he is a finnick over food: "If it's not too salty."

Running home after school he likes to help in the kitchen with the vegetables, the potatoes, or if it is near Christmas the ingredients of the Christmas cake which he is invited to stir and taste. He hears *O Sole Mio* on the radio and sings it to his mother, and mimics the sobbing passion of the Italian tenor, sinks down on one knee and

36

throws out his arms in entreaty, always delighted when she laughs. He brings home from the library a book of paintings and copies a picture with great care as a gift for her, hoping she will lavish praise on him, a Matthew Smith of arum lilies in a vase against a rich blue ground, criss-crossed with a scarlet wallpaper pattern. All she says is, "You're sticking out your tongue again, you funny boy." Hurt, his concentration total, he works on. All a waste. But later she finds a frame in a junk shop that is nearly the right size, fixing it in clumsily. He spies it one day, up on her bedroom wall. She will keep it for the rest of her life.

And he discovers the sea. Arrives in a charabanc with his family at a Co-op holiday camp outside Rhyl. There it lies on the horizon, his first sea, marvellous shining blade. An out-of-focus snap shows the o-p paddling in it complacently with rolled-up trousers, a knotted handkerchief on his head, but this is *his* sea, only his.

He is in a long wooden hut called a chalet, one of a dozen ringed around the edge of a dusty field, beyond it the sand dunes and the enormous empty beach. In the other direction brick toilets in a communal block, and a standpipe near the fence and the grass bank, where he goes with his father to fetch water in his canvas bucket, sometimes queuing for it. People smiling happily and chatting, children like dogs let off their leads. He marvels at the change in them all.

The sea, the sea. To feel the pull of it as it creams and froths around his toes. The vast expanse, how it glistens, almost oily with heat, swelling and pulling, a great serpent. His father wading into it with his brother on his back, who screams, terrified, screams so loud that it reaches his mother sitting far back on the beach. His father plodding on regardless, until his mother too is screaming, "Don't be a fool, stop it, can't you see he's frightened?"

"How could I," shouting, "when he's on my back!"

"Hear then – couldn't you hear him?"

"I had him, he's not even wet."

"Don't do it again, please!" his mother yells, red with heat, exasperation, worry.

To lie in the sweltering hut at night and hear his father tossing and groaning, his back badly burned. To hear again the story of his mother's mother, on holiday herself years ago at Rhyl with her family. A pitiful tale: getting off the coach and making wearily for the boarding house she sees a banknote on the ground and picks it up. A fiver. Carrying this huge find in her purse for several days, afraid of her very shadow. Should she give up this small fortune, should she keep it? God knows, they could do with it. The misery of this crisis of conscience ruins their holiday, even after going to the police station and surrendering it.

Chapter 6

He draws nearer to the great divide between his cosy, warm junior school, up from Miss Allen to Miss Shore, and then kindly, young Mr Edwards – only Miss Fellows who takes him for raffia striking a chill note, snappy and short-tempered, behind her on the wall a large framed picture of Jesus suffering the little children to come to Him – and the harsh world of retribution waiting in the big school on the other side of the city, in a district where he has never been. Innocent of this ugly threat, nearly eleven, suddenly the proud owner of his first bike, something he has longed for since the age of seven. It stands there gloriously on Christmas Day, propped against the kitchen wall in his Vecqueray Street backyard.

This fabulous apparition is a reconditioned machine but to him looks wonderful. Mudguards a glossy black decorated with twin gold lines that have been painted on by hand, the imperfections there to prove it. Nothing detracts from its preciousness, and with a glow around it because his father, not renowned for present-giving, has conjured it out of the air. Small, because he is. His father has struck a bargain, buying it from a shop in Hillfields specialising in the transformation of old cycles, all shapes and sizes. So wonder-struck he is, staring at it as if it had dropped from the sky. The one indisputably brand-new thing about this bike is its bell. How it shines!

First he has to learn how to ride, as hard as learning how to swim. His near-silent father takes him out to the deserted side streets leading to Humber Avenue, along the route taken on Sundays when he marches with his violin case towards Pinley Gardens, turning back when the level ground tips upwards. For a man capable of mad irritation his patience as a teacher is extraordinary. No traffic, as if warned away, as he wobbles forward with his father's steadying hand on the back of his saddle. Before long wobbling along unaided. Appears a troubled frown on his father's brow, as the bottom bearing begins to emit a persistent knocking sound. "Only a cracked ball bearing," he mutters to himself. "See to it later. Nothing to worry about." For him this extended speech can only mean that his father is concerned.

"See to it later," he repeats. Which he never does. Although able to tackle most things he is a clerk, not a mechanic. His father's pride in his literacy, his ability to compose fluent sentences, his clean collar and hands, his numeracy skills, all inform his critical attitude to Cyril and to the world. Cyril's musical gift has nothing to do with real life, and anyway his father is tone deaf.

On he goes with growing confidence on his bike, which gives him a feeling of superiority over mere pedestrians, suspended over the steady knock-knock which doesn't matter to him in the slightest. He is now in permanent love with his nearly new machine. And even being transported by it from Vecqueray Street to the fearsome reformatory school at Centaur Road doesn't feel like a betrayal of love. It obeys him absolutely, it is his only friend, it waits for him there. When each miserable day ends it carries him back home. It seems to know the way through the labyrinth of streets without him steering it almost, that faulty bearing with its familiar knock-knock like a consoling music in his ears.

Those infernal days are yet to come. Blithely ignorant, he goes off with his brother to spend a week of his summer holiday with Aunt Dorothy, his father's only surviving sister. She lives out at Brownshill Green with her husband Harry, a young plumber, an uncle he hardly knows. They have not long been married, and look at each other moonily, absorbed in each other and in the moonshine of their dream to have a home of their own, which they intend to build themselves on a plot of land half a mile away that they have already bought. Alas, the dream will founder for lack of money. He is taken to look at the site. Lined up at the wire fence they stare in at a lovely vision of deep grass and silver birch, a little grove like a bit of heaven. So pretty it is, flickering with birds, lush with promise. Green, green. The dream of the city man is always green.

"There it is, you've seen it," murmurs Harry as they turn away, back to the bare brick rented house that looks half empty, roomy but inhospitable, with no warmth burning at the heart of it like his. Even in midsummer his has a fire: it is where his mother cooks.

Dorothy puts a spell on him. She is mournfully beautiful. She stands like a brown stalk in the draughty space of the back kitchen at an ugly gas cooker, drooping there as if hoping to be rescued, from the smell of gas if nothing else. She glooms everywhere, in the kitchen and in the living room on the dark sofa, and if Harry is there he murmurs indistinctly, or is silent and stoical, or he takes his mandolin off the wall where it hangs like the half of a giant pear, its yellow curved back made of strips as if it is meant to float.

He loves the mellifluous word mandolin, and loves it more when Harry brushes the strings with his fingertips, lowering his head over it, pausing to answer Dorothy in his murmuring, muted way. Dorothy has the sorrowful pathos of the yearning romantic, with her dark looks, her long white neck, her white hands plaited together as she smiles sadly at them. Harry is consumptive, his hand jerking up occasionally to smother a cough. He has his own cup and plate, his own towel. Because of this, but not only this, he sees his uncle as someone set apart, by his illness, by his wistfulness, and somehow it is all expressed for him by the mandolin. He puzzles over some quality that he would call debonair if he understood the word. Perhaps his slight figure, his narrow chest, his high cheekbones and sunk, soulful eyes that twinkle whimsically now and then, and his subtle caressing of the strings of the mandolin are all part of it. At home he has heard them say that Harry can knock a tune out of anything. Twice a week he goes off to play in a dance band, sharp and small in patent leather pointed shoes.

Before he leaves, Harry goes over and murmurs to the inconsolable Dorothy. Their nephew-guest absorbs it all, the leavetaking, the mournful aftermath, almost liking the melancholy that lives in shadows in all the corners, touched into life by the magic of a few chords. Later he thinks of the endless gentle sweetness as something Harry has decided upon, wearing it like his patent leather shoes. Part of his charm. Was it really him, or simply assumed as a way of appeasing the soundless supplication of his beautiful dark wife, who in years to come will take her own life? He hero-worships his uncle's magician image, understanding nothing.

He still inhabits the false safety of his little street-corner Church of England school, three rooms in which he sits dreaming, half hearing the lessons, having the kind reproof written on his report – "He would do well if he did not daydream", a tiny world presided over by the fatherly, seldom seen headmaster Mr Harwood.

Feels repugnance for the boy who wets his corduroy short trousers, pity for Doris Petch, bone-poor and ragged with a snotty nose, and for Dennis Squires in his round steel spectacles, who stinks just like the stink in Squires' fruit and vegetable shop, which is like a dank cave dug into the wall at the base of the beetling cliff of the Morris building. His pity is like his mother's, it does no good and it makes him weak.

In Squires' shop the rough walls are running with damp, the low ceiling bulges down ominously, and on the blotchy walls are paintings Mr Squires has daubed himself on cardboard torn from cartons and nailed up with large-headed galvanised nails. When he goes in on errands there is no sign of Dennis. He can recognise crude silhouettes of swans on a stagnant, acid-green pool, a river the colour of Squires' carrots, trees like parsley, a lopsided sun that could have been sliced from a turnip, all in a phosphorescent glow. Portraits are overblown, with big swollen noses and heavy jaws, and when Mr Squires comes shuffling in from the back in his dirty brown warehouse coat he has the same round steel glasses as his son, the same pockmarked bulbous nose as those on his painted heads. He stands behind his boxes and says nothing, the glasses magnifying his eyes.

It is all coming to an end, he is about to be cast forth, out of the toy-like school and the street where he squats absorbed in the gutter to play marbles that he keeps in a linen bag made by his mother, with a draw-string to stop them spilling out. Opposite the school a fleapit cinema called *The Crown* where he is given a free bun and orange near Christmas, and the Parochial Rooms next to the school where he goes on special evenings to enjoy a cinematograph show on hard chairs, watching silent films that often snap in mid performance to a chorus of groans. Charlie Chaplin, the Keystone Cops, and one time the incomprehensible, engrossing *Birth of a Nation*, epic scenes of figures erupting in thousands, together with wars, earthquakes, revolutions, fires. Over from Miller's newsagents, that was called Mueller's until the Great War, on an area of cindery waste ground bordering the Gulson Road comes on bank holidays the triumphant gaudy roundabouts and stalls of Pat Collin's Fair, powered by great steam engines with trailing cables and flywheels that throb dangerously as if alive, alleyways festooned with blazing light bulbs. All about to end, and he has no idea. Lost in the thick crowd with his pennies, whirling round on the effigies of dragons and horses, the yelling gold and scarlet paint, the machine music, none of it to be the same again when he turns eleven. He will become scared and lonely, suffering a loneliness of spirit that seems without end.

Chapter 7

His agonies of shyness and his craven fear darken him with cowardice on his first day at Centaur Road School, and he is desolate beyond words, sick with longing for home, for all that has been torn away. He hears the tumult of noise from the playground swarming with boys before he turns into the road and approaches the iron railings. The school building is the biggest he has seen, of grey stone, three stories high, having nothing in common with his old school of red brick, small and shabby. It stands well back from the road and looks enormous, like a barracks. Inside the railings three slender trees are spaced out, and they seem to sprout out of the asphalt playground.

He walks blindly through the gates. Immediately a red-haired boy comes running across to him with something in his hand. He shouts, "Just starting?"

He nods dumbly. The red-haired boy wants him to buy his atlas. He holds out the tattered booklet, pages hanging loose, covered in blots and smudges. "I don't need this now," he says. "I had it off somebody when I started, and when you go up into Class 2 you can sell it." He is asked for fourpence, but he has no money. The boy runs off to collar another newcomer. Shaken, not knowing where to go, he begins to follow this other newcomer, keeping a good distance behind him. Struggling to fight back the tears of a coward, he feels speechless, struck dumb. Whistles blow, orders are shouted out: new boys this way, get a move on. Segregated, herded up prison-like stone staircases in a sinister echoing building and into a room on the top floor that is acrid with the stench of chemicals, to sit at scarred heavy tables fitted with sinks, and with bunsen burners attached to the gas taps by rubber tubes.

The teacher he will learn to refer to as Baggy Hall is introducing them to the school, with dire warnings interspersed. Stops in mid sentence. Waiting for him to continue, taking in his brutish appearance, the bullet head, cold glare, broad shoulders, thick black hornrims.

"Who's talking?" he asks, conversationally, as if enquiring the time of day, his voice cunningly tolerant, pitched low.

The roomful of unconvinced, stricken boys stays congealed in a common silence. He wonders if he will ever see again the small, thin figure of his mother, in another country, another world from this.

"He must have gone home," muses the teacher, and the word "home" cuts into him like a knife. "Never mind, you'll soon be home," his mother had told him hopelessly. "The first day's always the worst."

A boy laughs at the teacher's wit. It is the boy next to him, John Blasdale, a dopey, warm-natured farm lad, always bottom of the class, soon to be his one friend.

"Stand up the clown who laughed," invites Baggy Hall. His reasonable voice contradicted by a gruesome faint smile.

To his horror, Blasdale scrambles to his feet, red-faced.

"Something funny? Something I said?"

"No sir."

"Name?"

"Blasdale, sir."

"Sit down Blasdale sir."

John Blasdale lowers himself sheepishly, managing to scrape his chair. His unknown friend is filled with wild admiration for a courage he lacks completely, three parts stupid though it may be. You need imagination to be a coward.

"Let me just say," says Baggy Hall in his even, sinister tones, "that if a boy turns on a gas tap, believe me he'll wish he hadn't."

It crawls on, this morning that never seems to end. He reaches twelve at last, sneaking out of the hated iron gates and up the road to Hearsall Common. And tries in vain to comfort himself, to subdue his tears. A crab apple tree on the scrubby grass, looking as lonely as himself, seems as good a refuge as any. He climbs up and sits there, perched like a crow, forcing down the pulpy sandwich of tomato and cheese his mother has made in too much of a hurry. Everything she does is rushed, nervous. A slice of tomato slips out and falls to the ground, looking so dismal, like a bit of his mother, that he has to look away. He sits there as long as he dares, not knowing the time, in his blue shirt and misery, telling himself he is lost, outcast, the street he knows so well sunk out of sight behind a wilderness of roofs and chimney pots.

At home, when he is asked how he has got on, he says, "All right," the lie half choking him. He knows he has entered purgatory. Unable to tell anyone is his secret fate, hugging it to himself in bed, face buried in the pillow.

After a year, for some reason that he fails to understand, the school is transferred to Broadway Central Advanced, on the other side of Albany Road, a one-storey building with a curious design, all the classrooms opening on the same glass-topped walkway to create an open-air environment for young growing bodies. He has become a meek lamb, hoping to be overlooked, stiff with fear when a classmate is caned viciously, always one of the last to be chosen for team games. One bitter December, out on the playing fields at Memorial Park to play rugger, he ends up as full back because he is useless. All at once someone passes back the ball and he runs desperately with it instead of kicking it for twenty yards, cries urging him on, until a tackle round the ankles brings him down on the iron-hard turf. There is the brief haven of Christmas, warm and happy, before he is expelled into another stony January, cycling past those dreadful visions in house windows of Christmas trees and decorations, mocking reminders of a happiness dead and gone. Cold in Coventry.

He longs to be like the twins in his class, Cecil and Charles, both with dark hair and eyes, soft voices and cheerful pink faces. Whenever he glances over at them he thinks of rosy apples he has rubbed on his sleeve to make them shine.

Pupils are arranged in the classroom according to their term exam positions. To be placed in the front row is a disgrace. He sits there next to his friend John Blasdale, who clearly doesn't mind being branded a dunce. On the back row are the cleverest boys,

46

aware that they are singled out and can be trusted, sitting privileged with their backs to the brick wall. They are exempt too from the sarcasm and bad temper of teachers. He detests two of them in particular. One is dark, one fair. They are close friends, and one, called Greasley, is not only good at all subjects but brilliant at sports. Something compels him to look furtively at this hated boy's eager thrusting face, his smooth head of oily hair, his insufferable confidence.

In spite of himself he is fascinated by one teacher, a small, rather haughty man, impeccably neat. Wanting to be like him, admiring his straight back and springy step. His grey crinkly hair is perfect, like a wig, and the skin of his hands and face a hot brown. There is a legend that Mr Drake has lived in Egypt or China and is "cracked", but his admiration is unswerving. He imagines him trapped by a cruel fate in this small-minded school, too good for it, altogether too distinguished. He has a queer habit of twitching his hands and clutching savagely at the sides of his trousers as he teaches. He decides Mr Drake is too shrewd and humorous to be mad. Imagines him putting on madness as a mask, hating to conform completely. He snaps his fingers with a sharp sound and has favourite phrases that explode from him at moments of sheer exasperation, like "Buckets of blood" and "Ye gods and little fishes". He has darting, pale bits in his eyes, not cruel. Hardly ever still, he seems to have spasms of wild energy crackling through him. He spins round on his toes like a dancer in the middle of his stride and flings out an arm melodramatically, or cries out in a passionate, shaking voice, "Come out here, to the front, you foul thing you," his eyes bright with malice. He uses the cane sparingly, with obvious distaste. Occasionally he looks tormented, his face revealed for an instant as it really is, smouldering and bitter, and then his admirer's devotion turns to love.

He notices how Mr Drake dresses with great care, blowing his nose like a brisk trumpet, then stuffing the handkerchief back into his cuff with the corner poking out, exactly as it had been before. Everything about him is the essence of precision. He decides that when he leaves school and becomes a man he will dress like Mr Drake, in brogues and a light tweed jacket. Under the teacher's freezing, regal manner he detects a chuckling, kind person. As he marches up and down he breaks a stick of chalk into small pieces compulsively and rattles them in his hand like bones.

From the moment Mr Morris becomes his form teacher he lives under a cloud. He sees at once what is in store for him when he is faced with that neck and heavy head, the big hands with swollen-looking fingers, the bulbous forehead, the angry little eyes. Moggy Morris has a queer waddling walk like an overfed cat, but nobody laughs or imitates him in the playground. Even when he is nowhere near he inspires fear. In the mornings he feels sick at the sight of Moggy Morris's blunt burnished shoes. He sees them with dread out of the corner of his eye as he struggles with a problem.

Caning a culprit, he enjoys giving the boy a choice of canes, all of which look vicious, one or two with blackened ends. He hates this man so much that he has fantasies of revenge later on, snatching the cane from Moggy Morris's shocked hand and beating him round the desks. This is when he is strong, fearless, a man. While Moggy has power over him he is too mesmerised and helpless to do anything but submit. Those cunning eyes can burrow into him and uncover his thoughts, he fears.

One morning, the atmosphere of impending violence in the classroom is almost palpable. Except for the privileged back row, everyone sits cowed and bewildered. Moggy Morris's face is dark, and they know the signs. He is about to fly into one of his rages. After these ugly outbursts of passion the whole class sits as though stunned. No one knows what has caused such ungovernable anger, or indeed if there can have been anything known as a cause. It seems an eruption of blind fury for no reason, like an earthquake.

"I want to see your homework, get it out," he says, and goes straight to his desk.

He has never heard of this, nor have his classmates. The usual thing is for the homework to be collected and marked later in the day.

The teacher bends forward, hanging over his desk. "Not tomorrow," he shouts, "or next week – Now! Move yourselves. Quickly!" And his fist comes down.

48

A frozen silence after the blow, broken by hasty scuffling noises as exercise books are searched for in dangling satchels, placed in full view, open wide on the desk tops. The teacher walks up and down between the desks, leaning over one boy to see the work of his neighbour. Stops behind a boy in the front row, taps his shoulder and the boy jumps.

"Still idle, Edwards?"

"No sir."

"How many problems did I set you?"

"Yes sir, but –"

"How many?"

"Six sir."

"Out," Moggy Morris says, passing on.

Not hearing, or not understanding, Edwards sits still. The teacher wheels sharply, stabbing his back with his finger. "Out, out!" he yells, red-faced.

He stands behind John Blasdale. "What's this mess," he asks. "Expect me to read this?"

Blasdale grins sheepishly, mumbling incoherently.

"Ye Gods, the time I waste on you!" Stooping lower, he hisses softly in Blasdale's ear: "You still can't keep your work clean, can you? You still cover your homework book with blots and smears, don't you, even when you do any work?"

Blasdale, thinking he is being made fun of, smiles obligingly.

Losing his temper completely the teacher snatches the book, holding it at arm's length above his head, gripping one corner and letting the grubby pages flutter. "Have you seen anything like it?" he demands of the class.

Blasdale, under the impression he is being addressed, says, "No sir."

There is a shout of laughter. Moggy Morris flings the book away from him in a gesture of disgust. It hits the next desk and flutters to the floor like a wounded bird. "Out," he says, passing on.

Sitting beside John Blasdale he knows he is doomed. The pages of his homework book are blank. The problems he struggled with the night before were beyond him. "Out," the teacher says immediately.

As he stands up the teacher grabs his arm, pointing to a corner at the front. "We'll have you over there," he says, "all by yourself." Blasdale and Edwards are standing condemned by the blackboard.

One boy is shaken violently in his seat and told to wake up before coming to school. The colour drains from his face but he is left where he is. Moggy Morris goes back to his desk, lifts the hinged lid and draws out a long, pale yellow cane. It whips thinly in the air as he tests it out.

When Edwards is caned his fellow victim in the corner hears the whistling through the air, the loud smack on the palm held out quivering and naked like a tender leaf, and his heart shrivels and knots in agony as Edwards gasps snatching away his hand as if burnt to squeeze it under his armpit. His other hand claws at his waist.

He is next. The cane comes under his hand and pushes angrily upwards to straighten the fingers. His hand trembles uncontrollably. "Hold it still, or I'll give you a couple of the best," the teacher yells.

This time the hand is still but the cane misses, grazing the fingertips. Sometimes Moggy Morris misses on purpose, but not today. He staggers and almost loses his balance. His eyes blaze and he looks murderous. With his free hand he holds on to the bottom of his jacket. Raising himself on one foot he lashes downwards with all his shoulder's weight behind the blow. The cane crashes on the waiting flesh, his hand crumpling and disappearing beneath his armpit as if with a life of its own.

He sits with his teeth clenched, his crippled hand groping for the cold iron support of the backrest behind him. Hold on to the iron, they always say. It does nothing for the searing pain. His one act of bravery is to endure the pain without tears, only it is not bravery at all, it is yet more fear. Bursting into tears would be the ultimate disgrace.

Asked after the caning why he hasn't attempted the maths homework he struggles to speak but only gobbling sounds come out. The teacher is contemptuous. Once he had a nightmare where he tried to cry out, his mouth opening and nothing happening. For years after this failure to answer the teacher he looks upon himself as essentially speechless.

One boy whom the teacher takes pleasure in tormenting is Terence Dyer. He sits on the front row among the dunces, and can only grin like a half-wit when he is in a fix. Grinning when he is called out and caned, when he says something stupid and the class laughs, when the teacher ridicules him. Always an idiotic grin on his face. In the playground they sometimes form a circle around him, snatch off his cap and throw it from one to another, while he blunders after it, grinning. Someone gives him a violent shove in the back and he staggers from one side of the ring to the other. Nothing wipes off his silly permanent grin.

In the geography lesson one day the whole class has to learn and chant in unison something called Proofs of the Rotundity of the Earth. In a test later, Dyer writes: Proofs of the Root and the Tea of the Earth, and nothing else: he has forgotten the rest. When the teacher reads this out, the whole class erupts in laughter. Dyer grins. In future the teacher will say: Stand up, Dyer, tell us about the Root and the Tea. But he has had to write out the rest a hundred times after school, and now he has it. He begins:

One: all the other planets are round.

Two: during an eclipse the earth casts a circular shadow on the moon.

Three: men have travelled round the earth ...

At last he has it word perfect. He reels it all off and then sits down, grinning. But the teacher is unrelenting. At the start of each geography lesson he begins with: "Dyer, stand up." Somebody sniggers, though by now the joke has worn thin. "Somebody wake him up. Give him a poke in the ribs. Yes, you, Dyer. Who d'you think I'm talking to? You're supposed to do your sleeping at home. Stand up straight. Now, let's see if you still remember about the Root and the Tea."

Chapter 8

Unable for a second time to do his maths homework, he is distraught. He finishes two problems out of six, and even these are botched. Only a fool would consider them serious attempts. Moggy Morris, with his withering smile of pleasure as he draws out his favourite cane, the thin, springy one, will take one look and call out his name. The shame runs through his body as he pictures the scene.

He can only think of one way out, and that is to stay away, to disappear. To cease to exist. This preposterous thought is the measure of his despair. When they call the register and reach his name, no one will answer. Once he decides on this monstrous solution it seems the only possible one. But in the darkness of his heart, lying at night in his narrow bed, he knows that he has allowed the most shameful cowardice to take over his life.

His mother gives him his packet of sandwiches as usual and he puts them in his satchel against the horrible exercise books. A soft autumn drizzle blows into his face. He is alone. No one can help him. He begins the first of two desperate weeks as a truant, reduced to talking to his bike on meaningless journeys, silent one-way conversations that are at the same time all despair and yet sustaining. On his back the satchel bumping on his spine containing books he has stopped opening, together with his secret fate. Off to school, his mother believes. A liar and a fugitive. He waves goodbye, no one can save him now, he turns his face to the sickeningly empty street, the crucifixion of hours without end. One purgatory exchanged for another.

Ahead of him, at the end of his street, the colours fluttering down the traffic lights, orange and then green. This is the way he always goes. Instead, as soon as his mother is safely out of sight, he turns round and pedals in the opposite direction, towards the country.

His crime is too ghastly to think about, yet it blots out everything else. He will never be able to go back now, after this. Will his parents disown him when they find out?

He tries to pedal slowly to kill time, in the saddle all morning and on through the afternoon, from Gosford Green to Pool Meadow and up by a roundabout route to London Road Cemetery and on to Whitley Common, asking endless old men the time of day. "Can you tell me the right time, please?" The right time! Always the solemn reaching for the fob watch on its fat chain: there it lies like a landed sprat on the leathery palm to be studied and announced in such grave tones, sometimes in a croak, sometimes after much gravelly clearing of the throat. Querulous, watery eyes with sore rims focus on the time. "Thank you very much!" Thank you for nothing, for not noticing he is nothing, less than nothing – for not asking why he is not at school. Not that it matters to them – aren't they just killing time like him?

Certain he should now be getting home, he asks a woman going into a cottage. It is only three. There is a shower of rain. Shelters in the shallow porch of a house, until the door is snatched open and a thin staring man begins to come out. He walks across the pavement and rides off slowly, doing his best to look unconcerned.

He reaches home at the usual time. His mother asks innocently whether he has much homework, and for an instant he almost believes he has really been to school, that the whole day has been a dream. "Not too bad," he answers, the lie choking him. He realises how easy it is to deceive people who trust you: even your mother. He sites with his exercise books open on the table in shame and misery, pretending to write.

As day follows day he works up a pattern of calls, destinations and journeys, driven by sheer desperation. He thinks he must be the most timid rebel ever, pushing his bike obediently over the Common footpaths because cycling is not allowed. Stops at the cemetery and wanders around wretchedly until he reaches his grandmother's grave, the o-p's wife, who died when he was four. In far off happy days, so far off he is on the verge of tears, he would come here with his brother while the old man unwrapped his big scissors, emptied the rusty water from the tin vase and went to the tap for more, jamming in the stalks of a few bronze chrysanthemums, while he played tick round the blotched walls of a little chapel, leaping down the cracked steps by the enormous monkey puzzle tree with its great black drooping arms and bristling foliage, looking like a huge brush made of metal. It was all spikes, and ugly as sin.

He thinks he has hit on a refuge where he can spend hours. Surely in Woolworths and Marks and Spencers he can walk around all day in the warm and dry? He arrives at Woolworths too early for customers, only the bored shopgirls who notice nothing, though he has stuffed his cap in his raincoat pocket to avoid drawing attention to himself. The gaudy interior blazing with light like a palace. His face reflected in a wall of mirror glass behind the weighing machine startles him. Skin red from the rain and wind, the hair a high, black mop. He claws through his hair with his fingers, to flatten it.

He is in a fantasia world, a bazaar. A battering, man's voice singing, filling the space with noise. He feels less conspicuous as he understands that no one is taking the slightest notice of him. Gleaming counters stretching into the distance, smells that rise and mingle, heavy in the air, wave after wave of sweetness pressing round. He seems to be pushing through them with his face. Past the banks of sweets, greeting cards, Japanese toys made of tin, household goods. Round and round, trying to walk slowly, until he feels sure they must know about him as he studies the most unlikely goods, combs and collar-studs and cheap mirrors, tins of shoe polish, lace, elastic, handkerchiefs, cups and saucers, teapots.

Suddenly a panic grips him. They are about to ring a bell, viewing him suspiciously, about to call the manager. Saunters out like a real customer, unable to make up his mind. Out in the deserted street, bike propped at the kerb. He has used up no more than half an hour. Isolation is torture, and so is the drip-drip of interminable time. But no going back. Nothing to be done. He hugs his secret to himself like a leper. He longs to do what he most fears, let out the truth, confess, plead guilty, beg forgiveness. But in childhood there is no one to approach, and no end to time.

He finds himself one day in Spon End, a slummy, ashy area of cleared ground near the Coventry Chain factory and the Plaza cinema. Buildings torn down, alleys leading off the street lined with broken old sheds, doors hanging, decaying warehouses, defunct workshops that had been abandoned and left to rot, a stink of damp, the ground all potholes and hillocks. Not far away a new Technical College rising, made of buttery-yellow stone, covered in scaffolding but nearly built. Lifting into the sky like a vision, and though he has no way of knowing, this grand edifice fresh from the drawing board will be his salvation one day.

Like a rat in search of a safe hole he slips along a slot-like space, his bike bumping and shaking as he walks beside it. Comes to a halt at the end before a waste piece squalid with rubbish, cardboard boxes, ripped mattresses – a dumping ground used by householders. Stares at an ooze of water issuing from a brick wall that is adding to a wide shallow pool in an expanse of mud. The dripping water could be the underground Sherbourne, he thinks.

All at once a sun of hope shines in his chest. On a shelf of broken concrete a small boy hammers at some bits of wood, driving in a nail with a housebrick, around him a litter of cardboard and dirty scraps of newspaper. Desolate though the scene is, the urchin boy working with his back to him, the heels of his boots clotted with mud, looks cheerful rather than lonely, so absorbed he is in what he is doing. What is it? In a shower of rain he carries on as if he doesn't even notice. Edging up a little closer, and then the boy hears a sound and looks over his shoulder at him with his bike. Not in the least bothered, he bangs away with the half brick for a hammer.

Jimmy, he says, when he is asked his name. He tells him, not knowing why, that he doesn't go to school. The boy's pinched white face lights up. Hardly daring to believe in his good fortune he says to himself that he has an ally, they are fellow escapees. He looks anything but a hard case, but he hopes he doesn't look a sad one. He props his bike against a pile of rubble. He is just glad to stand physically close to this boy, feeling better about himself, less of a solitary outlaw and the loneliest being on earth. Wants to ask him how long since he stopped going, but asks instead about his bits of wood.

"What is it?" he asks humbly.

"Boat," the boy says, and goes on thumping away. So this is what he aims to do, sail across the stagnant water of the flooded ground in his own boat.

Even though the boy doesn't ask his name they are instant friends, he knows it. Thump thump, he goes, and it's a cheerful sound, resourceful, full of hope. Standing there a long time, relieved to be going nowhere hopelessly. Dares to ask if he'll be there tomorrow. Jimmy nods. Now he can think of leaving, and the next day is no longer a horror in prospect, a vast desert of time to be traversed with a feeling of sick fear.

"See you tomorrow," he says, and gets the same friendly nod. He would love to ask where he lives but that might alarm him, scare him away. Wheeling his bike off he still doesn't know what to do with himself, where to go, how to reach school-leaving time, but inside he is changed, in his chest a kernel of warmth. Another secret he must keep to himself.

Next day, there is Jimmy squatting on the fissured concrete as if he had been there all night, his bits of wood looking nothing like a boat. He does not want them to take on a shape: Jimmy might stop, with nothing else to do, and disappear. Fear clutches his heart. He understands that this boat is a dream boat; something to dream about. No older than his brother, the small boy is following his instincts, absorbed in a world of his own creation, his back to everything. Wonderful, he thinks, his proud little turned back. He dotes on him, on his very existence, with his spark of indomitable life.

Out again the following day, postponing his arrival at Spon End until the afternoon, though it pulls him like a magnet, sustained by Jimmy, by thoughts of him as he pedals along. The longer he can delay going, the shorter the enormous day will be.

Sitting on Whitley Common gulping down his mother's sandwiches, lumps of bread forced down over the guilt and fear in his chest, suddenly he can wait no longer. How good to be aimless no more, to have a destination that means something, speeding down the road with real purpose, legs pumping eagerly. The twinkling spokes of his front wheel, singing a song almost, bursting him out of a chain of nightmarish days that are suddenly wiped away. When he reaches the secret place and finds nobody, his eyes snatch at the scene as if unable to accept what they see. Is he somehow at the wrong spot? No, there's the water, oozing from the verdigris pipe in the middle of the dirty wall. No Jimmy. No bits of wood. He must have taken them and gone. Where to? Standing dumbly, his mouth open in a soundless cry: Jimmy! How could he have believed in him?

The tide of blackness which had been submerging him for days runs back in. Everything now looks hateful, ugly, and above all, hopeless. It mocks him: the wall, the water, the filthy rubbish. Feeling part of the debris and squalor, he turns round and retreats. The day which has lasted so long still has an hour to run. At the slot-mouth he looks back at the dreary hole, half expecting to see Jimmy. No, he's gone.

Arriving home, his face fixed to maintain the lie that goes on and on, he spreads his books out on the kitchen table for the homework that has long ago stopped existing. His mother calls to him brightly to tell him to clear away, the meal's nearly ready. Has it been two weeks, three?

His life as a runaway is ended without warning by a boy sent round from school to ask after him. He hears the weak knock, the small voice. Mouth dry, heart like a stone. One glance and his mother sees everything, his craven state, the dread his life has become. His father stands up violently, with a dark face, and orders him to bed. Lying in bed he hears an argument below, his father's voice raised in anger, the stairs door banging, his mother crying out, "It stands to reason he didn't do it for nothing!"

She takes him back to school herself. She holds his hand shyly, firmly, as if he has been lost, in a rare expression of the intimacy they have always shared. She says nothing, but her face says, "I wish I could go myself." Her diminutive figure already smaller than his. They sit in the headmaster's office, her own fear of schools and teachers miraculously overcome. Mr Wheeler is stocky and lame and has a nickname, Peg-leg. He is told to stand outside the door, while the low voices of his mother and the headmaster continue. When they come out, his mother leaves with hardly a glance at him, hurrying away across the blank playground. Before he has time to feel betrayed,

Peg-leg escorts him to his classroom. "Here's your missing boy – I'll have a word later," he says to Moggy Morris. He sits in his vacant place again, next to John Blasdale who is all eyes, feeling horribly naked in the front row.

What has been said about him? What does everyone know? In the break, when a few classmates come up and ask him where he has been, he says he was sick. No one calls him a liar. The teacher avoids looking at him, or else speaks to him differently, as if he is a special case. He wonders if others will notice this different treatment, and feels contemptible and exposed, like a favourite. After a few days his shame seeps away, and there are no reprisals.

It is Peg-leg Wheeler who takes them for singing, in the big draughty space of the assembly hall. His wooden leg, if that's what it is, is as fearsome as Long John Silver's in his imagination. "Stand up straight!" he orders, his cheeks inflamed by a strange rage, limping up and down in an ugly passion. "Open your mouths open 'em!" he bawls into stiff, submissive faces as they stand in a row like mouthing statues. Yet the rousing swing of *Camptown Races* excites him, as do the words of *Jerusalem*. In a fury the balding, inflamed man stamps up and down. "And did those feet" makes him nearly choke with frustration. He hops about, yelling, "Stop it, stop!" Gobbles at one boy, "Spell *feet*. It's got a 't', I can't hear the 't'." But the phrase that enrages him most is "arrows of desire". They go over it again and again, hissing like snakes.

He is still enthralled by the dazzling personality of Mr Drake, studying his face for signs of inner suffering, loving the regal wave of his right hand as he says, "Bring it here, dear boy." More than ever he sees him as a tragic figure.

One day, nearing thirteen, he gets wind of a possible escape from Broadway Central Advanced to the recently opened five-storey block of Coventry Technical College in Barker Butts, a new concept in education with its division into two halves, engineering and commercial. None of this means a thing, except that if he passes the entrance exam he will say goodbye to Moggy Morris and Peg-leg Wheeler for ever.

58

He must obtain the consent of his parents before applying. His father likes the idea of a college that specialises in the study of engineering. They live in a city of factories, and throughout the Depression he has had to suffer the handicap of lacking a trade. The sneers of Broadway teachers at the mention of "that jam-factory" down the road with its inferior standards and lax discipline only serve to drive him forward. The entrance exam amazingly easy, the letter of acceptance when it comes fluttering there like a bird of paradise. It is a moment of liberation he will always remember. He is out, he is free. It is a quiet triumph, resounding within him, one that only he really knows, and brought about by the work of his pen. In a flash of pure joy he sheds all his fear.

Chapter 9

His mother takes him worriedly to buy the school uniform, green cap and blazer and the purple and green tie, new flannel trousers. The same pang at the sight of her tightly held purse, her keen bony face determined to see him dressed well, counting out her pennies. Up through the streets and past the Baptist Chapel, and because of his release from bondage it all has a new face, people gazing at him with interest because, he thinks, of some visible change in him. Standing mutely in the Hertford Street outfitter's inhaling the musty smell as she fusses around him on this blue sparkling day. Is that a good fit? He is still growing, after all. The assistant fawning but pleasant, his words of comfort and reassurance, and he feels foolish and happy, hardly believing it has been accomplished with such ease, his prison break from those never-ending black days and despairing nights. His mother pays, the new outfit is parcelled up. Out in the bright street he once hated so bitterly, as he did all the others, he draws closer to her resolute little figure. Her debilitating anxiety about him which weakens him deplorably is forgotten: she is the force behind him. He is on his way.

Dawns the first clear day of his utterly new, misery-free life, the wind of change blowing through him. With nothing to fear, every step is an adventure, the excitement of the new world awaiting him making his heart race. Nothing is more nerve-racking to him than a first day, but this one is actually pleasurable. Sitting next to Stan Brown, small, neat and quick, whom he befriends, who lives at the top of Coundon, an affluent district. Sits in his unaccustomed relaxed state brushing against his friend's quiet confidence, his swift intelligent eyes, brown like his name, like his hair, a little confident smile flickering and going. He benefits from Stan Brown's alert assurance and any shred of nervousness melts away. This boy likes him. How astonishing to be appreciated, to be liked by someone so obviously bright. Confidence gaining by the minute, he is able to appreciate the dryly humorous, suave geography teacher, Mr Bloxham, with the silky moustache he must like, for he keeps touching it, who lobs pieces of chalk across the room at non-attentive boys, and to relieve his boredom. How good-humoured it is, with a complete absence of vindictiveness. There is Fritz the stiff-backed German teacher, Sparks the old man who teaches chemistry, abrupt and snappy with his ramrod back and peppery eye, his gaunt old profile from another age, but it is all impersonal, his snap and bark. Then the rarely seen headmaster, Whacker West, so-called because he is the only teacher allowed to wield a cane; red-haired, introducing himself at Assembly. Then in the afternoon, Miles the young English teacher, handkerchief in the cuff of his jacket, and soon in the coming weeks he feels sorry for him. The class rags him and he yelps helplessly at them, flustered and pink. And as if the reign of terror at Broadway had never been he wants Miles to inspire fear and regain control, unhappy at the sight of the man's self-respect in tatters.

Still in a state of wonder he wanders the corridors of this shining new palace of learning, its roll-up canvas blackboards, its lifts, even a buffet on the top floor; down below on the ground a theatre with cinema-like tip-up seats and raked floor where they assemble each morning. It will take some time before he stops feeling an imposter. With time to spare at midday he wanders into a narrow bookshop opposite the Council House, shelves of books to the ceiling on three floors, staring wide-eyed, oddly attracted without knowing why. On a table he picks up a book of paintings by Jack Bilbo, the name meaning nothing to him but he remembers it; the paintings luscious daubs, portraits of women in enormous hats, primitive dancing figures, the colour swirled about with large brushes. Another day he goes to open it surreptitiously and look again.

Going home at dinnertime for a snack to shabby, curiously shrunken Vecqueray Street, his world suddenly expanded. When his mother wants to know about Stan Brown, where he lives, what he looks like, all he can think to say is, "He's small, he's nice," reluctant to give in to her inquisitiveness.

In metalwork he has to wear a boilersuit, bought cheaply by his mother in the market, which he stows away afterwards in a metal locker with a key. He shrugs into it with difficulty, struggling with the strange garment, its coarse heavy-duty cloth and stiff creases, not liking the hard-to-fasten metal-buttons, or of the way it turns him into something alien, a clumsy oaf, dark blue like a beetle. Stands at a bench filing at a lump of steel in a vice, and here is his first taste of the world of work to come, the grim and purposeful domain of industry looming, around him the lathes and millers in imitation of a real workshop, the teacher in his white coat with hands dug in his pockets, scowling at their mistakes, stifling his derision, once a tradesman himself, a man who has been to evening classes and bettered himself, now an instructor in this pretend-workshop, hands itching to do a man's work.

In the woodwork class his new linen apron gives him a different feeling, the wood smell is kindly and wholesome as steel never is, yet it is make-believe: he knows he won't be a carpenter. The tall, lean teacher has a personality that is somehow in keeping with the living tissue of wood. He is mellow and philosophical, as if in touch with an age-old tradition, before the birth of industry, even joking with his pupils when he is in the mood. "What is it?" he asks in mock bewilderment as he examines one boy's attempt at a dovetail joint. "What's it supposed to be?"

He likes the atmosphere but can't take the subject seriously. At the end of his first term he takes home the medicine chest he has made laboriously, its joints ill-fitting, and presents it proudly to his mother.

Afterwards he looks on this period as a carefree interlude, between the servitude of hated Broadway and the approaching servitude of an occupation, which no one mentions, any more than there is mention of sickness and death. It seems that no sooner has he got used to it all, become part of it, excelling at subjects in which he was regarded as useless before, than it is drawing to a close. Nearly two years have flashed by. And before it ends, with one term to go, the war declared. Uncle Bill calling in at home and the political discussions with his father have thrown up names like Haldane, Stalin and Hitler, Bill airing his knowledge about the war in Spain, its use as a training ground by Germany and what's been learnt about the effects of bomb blast, how it can hurl you to the ground from hundreds of yards away, smash your windows. His mother's scorn, arguing with his father who sticks stubbornly to his opinion, in agreement with his brother, saying that it is so, yes. "What does Bill know?" his mother demands. "Has he been there, in Spain?" Her angry eyes, hot cheeks. "Of course not," his father says, turning away from the woman whose ignorance of world affairs has nothing to do with his view of her, back to his paper full of male certitude. And soon he is enrolling in the ARP.

Yet on weekends in the Indian summer nothing changes for them as a family, except for the unreal shadow cast by the threatening war. He is growing, full of young eager life. These phantoms conjured up by adults mean nothing to him. Still mounted on bikes as a family, cycling three abreast through the lanes towards the south, Warwick and Stratford, never northward. Arriving yet again at the camping site outside Stratford where the brown, slow river flows eternally against the meadow, the great umbilical cord to which they feel fastened: the big tent with the fly-sheet unpacked, rising triumphant, a small tent for him and his brother, and the cooking equipment, the bedding, all sent on ahead by rail. Once driving up in style in a Morris 8 tourer that his father has borrowed from his firm, with he and his brother sitting chirpy and bright in the rear like birds in the nest.

Mornings of yellow sun with scarves of mist lifting from the river, delious smells of bacon frying on the limpid air. Now and then joined by Cyril and his friend Wal Handley, goggled and gauntleted on a giant Triumph machine. The makeshift diving board rigged up, simply a plank and ropes in the fork of a willow tree, his father diving off in fine style but forgetting to remove his glasses. Down go his father and Cyril to salvage them, groping round on the muddy river bed in vain. The story goes into a gathering collection of family legends, along with the farm goat at Barford, the canoe Cyril builds in his garage at Pinley from a Hobbies blueprint, templates drawn on brown paper and transferred to plywood, the plywood shaped and slotted to fit over the long keel of ash, Bill coming over with his newly acquired upholstery skills to stretch and tack hessian, hammer snapping at incredible speed, his mouth full of blue tacks. Then the coats of glue size, then the six coats of paint. Finally the canoe's journey lashed to the top of Cyril's solid-tyred Trojan to the Avon for the launch. Floating there in apparent triumph, but unstable, rolling dangerously. He watches as they take it back grimly to fit stabilisers.

Always on these camps his mother transformed, turning brown like a gypsy, smiling as he rarely sees her smile at home, the space and freedom working their magic, clothes loose and light-coloured, headscarf knotted gaily as though in response to the sunny naked field, the living brown body of the river flowing. Even the chores she hasn't escaped fail to make her frown, the cooking improvised on the Primus, his father fetching water from the standpipe in his canvas bucket, washing enamel plates and tin pans at the river's edge with handfuls of grass and grit, the ex-army man in his element. His reward is to stand for hours on the river bank fishing, still and silent as a tree. When the soft purple twilight gathers he stays on, like a sentry. When his son is sent to fetch him, the father has it seems been struck deaf and dumb. No answer. Then one evening he erupts into violent life – he has hooked an eel. Two feet in length, it tangles his line in slime. He calls harshly for the landing net like a sergeant: "Quick, quick!" Bulging with muddy force, the eel writhes on the grass. His father kneels to it, while he stares petrified at the sight of this monstrous underworld truth.

Chapter 10

Back to college, to be told they are to be evacuated, but only a mile or so away and only for English and Metallurgy. How that will save them if the bombs fall becomes a joke, and so afterwards is the one he hears at home, a theory that Coventry would be hard to find because in a hollow. Nothing happens, but he loves the novelty of trailing out to the fringe of Memorial Park to sit in big wooden huts on bare boards in a stirring excitement at the unfamiliarity.

Then one morning a forlorn muddle of little children assemble in the road outside the college for real evacuation, including his brother, though he is snatched back at the last moment, reprieved by his mother who thinks better of it. A mild sun sweet in the sky above these fraught mothers and children. Whacker West there with his bullnosed Morris, for what reason he fails to understand. Solemn mothers huddle in clusters and discuss frantically, small boys wander about with pathetic suitcases, not knowing whether to cry or be pleased.

Then all at once the upheaval comes closer, into his backyard. His father signs a paper importantly, taking delivery of the galvanised iron ribs of an Anderson shelter. No decision, because already decided, how to instal it and where. Outside, on his way to college he stares at the pieces, wheels his bike around them. For a few days they are left to stand there, propped against the brick wall of their outside lavatory, where a year ago (his mother having decided he should be told the facts of life, distasteful though the task must have been for her) he was sent to read what she had scrawled on a scrap of paper: the man puts his thing into the woman's thing, to make babies. "Now throw it down the pan and pull the chain." Down it goes, that incomprehensible dirty secret.

The eight by eight backyard is about to become a building site: everything, the sooty flower border at the base of the splintery fence, another fence of trellis on a frame in front of the lavatory, nasturtium tendrils using it for support, with their peppery seed pods he puts in his pea shooter to aim at his brother. He finds it hard to believe that this flowery oasis his father has tended, watered and weeded, filling the nose on summer evenings with something other than the rancid dairy stench wafting in on certain winds, is now due for demolition.

Weird to see his father seemingly unmoved, his stoical pale clerk's face, springy black hair and little Charlie Chaplin moustache giving the same impression of immovable purpose that his tail bony figure always conveys. And those big hands, that he fears and respects.

Down comes the trellis with a crash, then the plants and flowers forked out, the big clump of Michaelmas daisies excavated by the gate. "These instructions are for if you're gormless" he says to Cyril on Sunday, handing over the official form, and they set to work. Cyril has come in his car, bringing a pick. His father has his treasured trenching tool, and spade and fork. Rain sprinkles down ignored. His father civil to his brother, he notices, because he has to be, though there is no doubt who is in charge. Before Cyril can take off his jacket and rolls up his sleeves his father starts digging at the black ashy soil, unearthing clinkers, broken pots and dog bones, left by previous tenants. The rectangular hole sinks down rapidly, earth piled into buckets and spilled against the fence. Rain falls fitfully on the rubbish and the labouring men, on the stricken-looking ground.

"Come inside a minute, you'll get soaked," calls his mother in vain, then as the rain eases she comes out with mugs of tea. "What a job, oh look at it, such a mess, I hate it," she moans, nobody listening. He would like to join in but there is no spare spade and no room. He imagines doing it, in a hole getting deeper by the minute. Would he feel like a gravedigger? He is told to make himself useful and put some plants in a bucket. He asks his father to say where he should put them and is told, "Use your brains." Cyril, ordered to do this and that, obeys submissively but with a languid air that slyly contradicts his father's authority, flicking glances at his mother to see her reaction. At any moment he expects to hear from his father the sentence he hears everywhere, usually as a joke: "Don't you know there's a war on?"

The hole at last down four feet, the regulation depth for an Anderson. "That's it." His father straightens his back, groaning. In go the curved ribs to be bolted together, and now in his mind's eye he sees an edifice as huge as a whale, gleaming, all newness and importance. When Cyril is gone, the front and rear sections in place, his father inside the house, he peers into the dark earthy tunnel with his brother. His father comes out and orders them away. He intends to work on, though it is getting dark. His mother reappears to beg the weary construction worker to stop, to have a rest. "You'll do your back in, don't be so pig-headed."

"Tell that to the Jerries," he mutters, now totally in the grip of his obsession. With timber gathered beforehand, cheap off-cuts from a yard he knows, he hammers together a slatted floor on joists, a frame entrance, and hangs up a roll of hessian for a door, complete with tapes sewn on by his mother. Next morning he gets up for college, but his father has been up for hours shovelling back the earth on to the bowed back of the shelter before going to work. Finds rocks in no time and has the rudiments of a rockery up there, a final act of ingenuity to appease his mother. Soon plants and bits of heather are trowelled in between the rocks. His mother abashed, feeling bound to acknowledge this homage to a growing world that defies the skies, if not the gesture to herself. She says meekly, "Aren't you clever." Propped on his spade, the proud creator pretends not to hear. They stand together, silently at rest for a moment, gazing at this proof of love.

After three months of a war that refuses to begin, later called "phoney", listening to Tommy Handley on the battery radio, he leaves college. He is fifteen, and accepts unquestioningly that his father has plans for him. His letter-writing, ending as it always does with "Thanking you in anticipation" when a firm is being approached, has borne fruit. He is intent on securing an apprenticeship with a prestigious company for his son. Neither his mother nor his father ask if this is what he would like, and if they did he would have had no answer. Going along with their wishes is for him an act of filial duty.

The deed is soon done. Innocent of everything he is delivered by his father to the Coventry Gauge and Tool Company to be enrolled as a toolmaker apprentice, as it happens on Fletchamstead Highway, opposite the Standard where his uncle Cyril works in the dead of night. Entering the gates to be interviewed, he understands at once what attracts his father to this live, desirable, humming factory. It is something he would have wanted for himself: a trade. In the concrete blockhouse where the works police kill time, airless, windowless, fetid with tobacco smoke and sweat, he waits with his tense, expectant father for the arrival of the Apprentice Supervisor, Mr Scannell, who has to be telephoned. Bursting through the door as if he has not a minute to lose, his white butcher's smock stained at the pockets with industry, the grime of iron filings in his fingernails; in his hand the papers to be signed by his father, who has gained immeasurably in importance because of the occasion, asking pertinent questions before he puts his name to anything to show that he is no fool, he is aware of the small print of these matters.

It is explained to the boy apprentice-to-be what the word indentured means. Meekly compliant, he nods, torn between pride in his father's dignified stance and embarrassment at the stilted, cold scene of confrontation. He dislikes Mr Scannell on sight, his long sceptical nose, his North-country voice grey with duty and rules, his curious sideways-working lower jaw like a sheep's as he reels off his prepared speech, leaden with false gravity. His father tries to raise a point but is swept aside by Mr Scannell now in full flow, lugubriously emphasising the advantage, not to say privilege of six years in the care of his company, at the end of which his son will have a trade to be proud of, and be a freeman of the city. Excluded from this monolgue he cannot help staring at the man's nicotine-stained, spaced-out front teeth, his knobbly wrists thick with black hairs. This company, Mr Scannell concludes, his large eyes pale and dead, is famous the world over for its precision tools, out to intimidate his father who stands his ground stubbornly and considers. Piqued, Mr Scannell pushes the official document of indenture forward, with a pen. Still his father hesitates. Pulls out his own pen, decides to read the whole rigmarole again. He stands squirming. Then his father signs. On January 1st his six-year sentence will begin, when he reports in person to this self-important, humourless man. He hopes his aversion to him will lessen in due course.

Turning to the boy as they are about to leave, he asks, "Are you keen, son?"

"Yes sir."

"Not afraid of work?"

"No sir."

"Good, good."

Hanging there, slack at the knees, chest caved in, the top pocket of his white coat bristling with pens, pencils, gauges.

Outside, a copy of the indentures stowed away in his jacket, his father looks pleased and flushed, telling him, "Seems a decent sort of chap, I thought. Straight-talking, no nonsense about him."

Chapter 11

His first work day in the great world, a bleak January morning. Nervous, he sets off earlier than necessary, wanting to make a good impression. Pedals off down the street he is always leaving, smiling off his mother, sick as ever inside with apprehension. His mother there to wave encouragingly, as if she knows, can see inside him, and it is true, she always knows. The old question: is it him she grieves over her or herself? Off across the city, along Ford Street, past the public baths and the Hippodrome, past the new cinema called the Rex in Corporation Street, up towards Earlsdon and that common with its lone crab-apple tree, then the slow haul of Tile Hill Lane until the intersection, the big sweep of the four-lane motorway of Fletchamstead Highway with its cycle track, an unheard-of thing. He rides along it self-consciously, the only user. The factory as he approaches it looks big and squat, larger than he remembers, modern, with its saw-tooth profile.

Nothing worse than being a beginner, ignorant, out of place. The facade of the factory ends and there is Torrington Avenue at the side and the railway to Canley one way, Birmingham the other. Finds the rear entrance, guarded by works police in another concrete pill box with slits for windows. Asks for the cycle sheds and instantly feels a fool because as he opens his mouth he finds himself looking at them. Upends his bike in a rack and fastens it with chain and padlock. All the omens seem grim. Asks a surly man in a boiler suit for the Apprentice School; the man continues walking while he keeps up with him. Points the way without bothering to speak.

Strange, cold, a mechanical no-man's land into which he has to fit. Low sheds stretching ahead endlessly, past holes in walls, open doorways, letting out an acrid smell. Inside one interior he catches a glimpse of a square orange fire, and sees dark burrowing figures. Ahead of him comes a man in a filthy boiler suit, pushing a barrowful of steel cuttings. The steel ribbons are brown and purple and in rapid spirals, short and long pieces, tangled like snakes in a high swaying heap.

He thinks he may have taken a wrong turn. Goes along the side of a pool of stagnant water, about twenty paces square, edged with tubular railings, the surface coloured and veined with oil. Sees a sign. Opens a door on shrieks, groans and clanks, massive broaching machines in long identical lines, bluish fog hanging over them, with occasional handfuls of white sparks jumping out from the rims of grinding wheels. Long shafts of broaches are being dragged through blocks of tortured steel. Men with oily hands looking up angrily as he passes down a gangway, or perhaps just curious, girls with hair tucked under mob-caps staring brazenly, one nudging another.

Stepping out of this inferno he is astonished by the Apprentice School because it looks so small and orderly, in a flood of fluorescent light. It is really a pen in a corner of the shrieking shop floor, fences topped with wire mesh segregating it as a miniature toolroom, lathes, millers, drills, a jig-borer, shapers and benches, the workforce all boys learning the basics of their trade. Beyond this compound lies the throbbing men's world, operators calling across to each other, letting out jeers, catcalls, guffaws above the din, now and then a chorus of wolf whistles. He thinks afterwards of walking on to a stage set, remembering a play he has seen at the college theatre. Nothing real, but there is Mr Scannell the supervisor in his glass booth as if taking refuge, looking somehow beaten down. He jumps up, and winds his fingers together like a vicar.

Suddenly animated, he waves in his two assistants for him to meet. Mr Baldwin slips in first and steps aside unctuously for his colleague, then lounges in the doorway, insolent, eyes wary like a professional gambler. His white coat stained with grease around the pockets, hands dug in out of sight, his air of "Don't ask me". With sallow, pock-marked skin, the frayed ends of his trousers dropping on his heels, a black thinned-down moustache, black hair glued flat on his scalp, parted as if by a steel rule. Not looking at anyone, not at Mr Scannell, never at him, gazing up at the roof trusses and his mouth faintly amused, as if to say it is all playacting, a joke. Mr Jackson is nothing like this, shouldering in like a bull, crude and shambling, a thick neck and his head sunk down, hair in a brutal gingery crop. Little pig eyes, coarse mouth, but the same air of "Don't ask me".

He understands that this is a nursery and these chargehands are nursemaids, wet-nursing boys because it is a soft number, has status and pays better. Swearing is against the rules. The youngest apprentices call them "sir". With little to do they gaze through the mesh at the haze of blue smoke over the big howling machines outside as if yearningly.

Handed over to Mr Baldwin he is glad to be assigned to him, and relieved to get away from the crushed man in the glass box who sits hunched at his desk holding his head in his hands. These two assistants who clearly feel contempt for the supervisor with his endless paperwork are perhaps why he appears beaten down. Apparently they have joined forces against him. Mr Baldwin with his degraded, soiled appearance and his corrupt-looking mouth changes into someone friendly and likeable when he speaks. Cynical to the core, he clearly cares nothing for the high standards preached by the supervisor. He is there because it suits him, suits his cheap style. He acts like the teacher he is supposed to be but takes pleasure in his favourites, boys who joke with him and admire him. Walking about and lounging, standing against a boy in almost indecent intimacy and whispering in his ear; a local hero. Smoking is also against the rules but he sees Mr Baldwin light up and puff away in a corner, out of sight of the supervisor. "Don't let me catch you smoking," he says, soft as a thief, to one of his hero-worshippers. "I can but you can't." The current word for him is "spiv", his pencil-thin black moustache is pure Hollywood. He is reminded of George Raft. Mr Baldwin's oily voice fascinates him, as does his falsely urgent scurry when the phone rings and it is for him. Studying him, he sees that his actor role is self-created. There is something funny in the way he makes it seem illicit, with his little circle of favoured apprentices for audience.

Next to the supervisor's office is a schoolroom, for basic talks on safety and the care of machines and tools, standard practices displayed on the blackboard for him to jot down and remember. Feeling outlandish in his khaki warehouse coat he is put to work on a bench lathe that looks like a toy. Indeed he is in a toy domain. There is a miniature stores with a boy storekeeper in charge. Mr Jackson fastens a small length of steel into the chuck of his lathe and skims along it with the tool, showing him how to measure the diameter with the micrometer belonging to the School, telling him like a threat that he will have to buy his own. When the tool becomes blunt he follows Mr Jackson like a lamb until the instructor decides to listen, swinging round his bull shoulders. "Get the bloody thing out and bring it here, it won't walk by itself." He loathes the man's voice and everything about him, but can only submit. Back again with the blunt tool. Taking his time, Mr Jackson goes over to the grindstone, stabbing the green button with his stubby finger. He stands obediently, eyes on his ginger neck, while sparks fly upward from the whirling stone. "Now you know," Mr Jackson says, though he hasn't understood.

Somebody tells him he is working behind an Austrian refugee they call Fritz. He is a Jew. His name is Franz. He bends short-sightedly over his work. His neck rises up long and stiff, and his speech is stilted. One afternoon he hears a commotion, Jackson telling the tall unsmiling boy that his work is scrap, he has cut too much off. His voice malignant, Jackson says, "You dozy sod." The foreign boy bursts into years. Disgusted, Jackson moves off muttering, "Christ." Behind, he stands frozen and horrified, the commotion now in him, bleak inside, both for himself and for the boy standing friendless, others looking on curiously. Watches as Jackson returns with another piece of steel and drops it down. "Think what you're doing." In his mind now the thuggish Jackson is the enemy, and the slippery Baldwin attractive. Baldwin sidles, ingratiates, but in his low tricky voice there is a kindness. They are a kind of double act, exchanging glances over the heads of their flock of novices. He is reminded of prefects at school, their preening, their proprietary air. The little power they have has long ago been found boring.

The boy who intrigues him from the very beginning during his initiation at the School has a strange surname. He first sees it on his clocking-in card: Xerri. You pronounced it to sound like sherry. Don Xerri has a well-off family and a boarding school voice, his pale pink skin incongruous in a factory. The languor of his gestures belongs to another realm entirely. He giggles, pretending to be industrious, and for some reason he is never criticised. There is a glamorous sweetness about him. If he laughs, it is a soft explosion of sensuousness, opening his mouth and stretching his throat, showing his hard white teeth. Xerri is one of two boys hanging back one morning after a talk in the schoolroom on precision instruments, their care and use. He glances back puzzled to see them cuddling against the wall, Xerri subtly touching his friend's cheek, smiling his secretive smile. The long-faced, lugubrious supervisor has retreated to his glass booth. "See the two nancies?" he hears someone say, and doesn't catch the sniggering reply. Do they mean girlish? He is none the wiser. Clearly it is something to be mocked. All the same he envies their warm amorous contact, the flow of affection.

Home at the end of the first day, pale and tired-looking, so his mother says, legs aching from the long hours on his feet, he is asked what it is like. "All right," he says, but the question is impossible to answer. Goes to bed early, pedalling again early next morning for the place that is like nothing he has ever known, where a card has to be punched in a time clock, where you sit in a dismal shed with benches against the walls eating your sandwiches and your Lyons fruit tart if it is raining, or walk out on the highway to sit on the grass verge, trucks thundering by. Speaks to no one, listens to others talking. Nervous of being late, arriving back at the School too soon. Empty space, dead machines. Outside the compound they are still working, the broached rings shriek and groan. Two girls peer in through the wire, egging each other on. Go off tittering together. Lonely, he longs for home. Takes the hated warehouse coat off his hook, wears it. The yellow buttons held on with split rings. The garment makes him feel convict-like for some reason. Stands still and waits for time to pass. A nameless boy saunters in. The time clock says ten minutes to go. Mr Baldwin is in his cubbyhole, smoking furtively in his cupped hand, his back to everything in his grubby white coat like a rat in its hole. He goes to his bench lathe and conceals his true feelings as best he can. What if the expression on his face is giving him away? He hopes it is not saying that the pain of confinement in this ugly place is urging him to run off.

He wonders about the blackboard fastened to the end wall of the classroom, which has rubbed-out chalk marks visible on it but is apparently not used. The whole point of the classroom, he is beginning to realise, is so that the company can boast of their progressive treatment of apprentices when visitors are shown round. Then one morning a plump, dynamic little Russian arrives, middle-aged, a bald dome pushing through his thinning black locks, which hang over his ears in oily rings. Older apprentices call him the Professor. He runs a private school for girls and visits once a month. The man's passion is mathematics.

He sits near the back of the small class, at first sceptical and bored. Although he passed his final college exam at fifteen with a distinction in maths, he has no idea how he achieved this. All at once he is hanging on to the Professor's words. The foreign little man with a thick accent speaks so ardently that he is disappointed when the session is over. The Professor's fire has inspired him with a desire to taste the almost mystical satisfaction of pure maths. He hears the gospel of Calculus, Differential, Integral, Infinitesimal, all preached with rapture. Euclid is described as an art in itself, its abstract qualities akin to that of music. The rigorous, passionate little teacher is trying to raise him up, he feels, to ignore the chaos surging at the windows. The purity of his subject affects him like a religion. When he comes a month later and has to lecture on practical applications, the cutting edges of tools, the varying angles of drill points for different materials, the Professor's lack of enthusiasm is obvious, he can tell. Though he doubts if he will ever master it, he longs for the rapture of pure maths again.

After two months on various machine tools, including a week on a fitter's bench, he is posted out for his baptism in the main shop, a vast area of factory floor divided into sections, with machines of all sizes lined up along gangways indicated by white lines painted on the boards; a Press Tool section with an aristocratic air, a War Department, an Admiralty Department. Huge planers, towering radial drillers, a huddle of capstan lathes worked by women. Precision thread grinders, automatic machines with their tools operating in thick curtains of oil, their operators attending them like slaves. A fenced area where the inspectors sit. Motor trollies trundling back and forth, men hanging over the counters of stores, using numbered brass tokens for coinage. Some of the driving power for this plant is electric, and some machines are still driven by a system of overhead shafts and pulleys, with flapping belts engaged by pushing over a great tongue of vertical wood.

Reporting to the turners he is assigned to one of these, an old belt-driven lathe that looks ancient, no doubt suitable for an absolute beginner such as himself. He accepts his ignorance and inferiority, standing before the foreman, who takes him over to the machine and consoles him brusquely. "Don't break your heart over it, this is only temporary. I'll put you on something better in a week or two." This busy, clever-looking man who speaks so rapidly and quickly departs has misunderstood his expression. He has no ambition whatsoever. "Any problems, see Bert Satchwell," he says over his shoulder. Satchwell is the chargehand.

There is nothing difficult about his new job, but he soon finds himself in trouble. By the side of his machine is a heap of cast steel bars. They are scaly, brown-coated, their skins horribly tough. He is to get them ready for the skilled turners by making a few rough cuts, peeling away the tough rind. He is told not to bother about measurements.

He fastens in the first heavy bar and pushes over the long wooden starting handle, feeling primitive, back in the nineteenth century. Up near the roof the belt slithers and screeches, then gives a final piercing scream and the chuck of his machine comes alive. The bar spins round. He daubs on a brushful of suds from a tin can and edges up the wedge-shaped tool. He is too timid, and the tool only rubs. He presses harder, burning the tip of the tool; it has made no impression on the scale. Discouraged, he unscrews the tool and goes over to the grindstone to resharpen it.

There is a man already using the stone. The heavy wheel roars softly inside its fat casing, which is trembling, as the blurred rushing edge flings off orange sparks in spasms. Watching, he is nervous of its size and weight: it is twice as big as the one in the Apprentice School. The thin crouching man sways his body before it like a knifegrinder he had seen once in the street as a small boy. He stops abruptly, straightens up and plunges his hot smoking metal into a tray of gritty water. The water hisses and steams, then grows a grey scum.

It is his turn. The surface of the stone is lumpy. His tool bounces and clatters against it. He is afraid that if he presses too hard it will wrench out of his hand. He has heard lurid stories of such things, the stone cracking, exploding in all directions.

He is glad to finish. Still it is no good. Bert Satchwell is a short, stout man, round-shouldered, with a squint. He goes up to him meekly and tells him his problem. Half expecting to be sworn at, he is listened to by this man who is virtually dumb. Unlikely as he is, he becomes his first factory hero. Already he hopes to please him, to have him nod with approval. When Satchwell does speak he is touched by his shy reserve. "Where you workin'?" he mumbles, staring down at his shoes.

He walks behind the chargehand, who half waddles, half rolls along like a sailor, throwing out his feet.

He is taken back to the grindstone and shown how to grind a better angle on the tool. Back at the machine he watches while the man throws over the starting handle, winds up the tool and digs in hard, under the hard skin, chips of hot steel flying up. Flicks off the bits falling on his hand. Stops, reaches for a spanner to adjust the tool. Digs in again, turning to him. "Whatever you do, don't nibble at it," the man mutters. "Take a good bite." For Bert Satchwell this is quite a speech.

Left alone, he is initially more confident. Chips of steel leaping hot for his face and eyes. Frantically he knocks them off. Hot, stinging. One glues itself to the back of his hand and has to be plucked off, leaving a red mark. Even on this simple job there are things to learn. Soon the tool is bucking, skidding, refusing to cut. Goes looking for Bert Satchwell, admiring the skill of his puffy red hands. Never hurrying, woollen belly hanging over the bed of the lathe. Over with him again to the grindstone. Again he is started off. He takes comfort in his hero's slow, sleepy body, which nothing on earth seems to trouble. He longs to be like him, to win his praise.

Goes on skinning the long bars, this time with more success, ploughing off the dark crusts and dropping each bar of steel down newly naked on a warm pile on the suds-soaked floor. They look sleek. Twenty in a heap on the floor by the time the hooter goes for dinner.

Life is a little better, and more real now that he has shaken off the weird hot-house atmosphere of the Apprentice School with its artificial seclusion. Nothing to say when he reaches home but he knows that something has changed inside him. He has got older suddenly, no longer a schoolboy, standing there alone among men, in a multitude of men. His first pay packet at the end of the week, eleven and fourpence, he hands over proudly to his mother, and she gives him pocket money. His legs still ache from the long hours of standing up when he goes to bed. His brother, still secure in his childhood, seems a million miles away, though they still chatter in the bedroom as if nothing has happened.

Chapter 12

So his war has started. The war with Germany that they are calling phoney is irrelevant, the Anderson shelter hasn't sheltered anyone, only ration books and the blackouts are different, traffic creeping past at night with black slitted cowls over their headlights.

The first casualty is his grandfather, coming back stone-deaf at night with a carrier bag of thrillers from the Central Library. Knocked down in pitch dark Trinity Street near Owen Owen department store by a van that doesn't stop. Gathered round his hospital bed he stares at the old man lying unconscious, strangely peaceful-looking, seemingly without a mark on him. Why doesn't he feel upset by his grandfather's accident? He tells himself he will get up soon, sit up and ask for a cup of team, if it really is him lying there. Then dead within hours, as the family sit quietly by the fire at home and he stares at where he should be, in his own armchair. His mother silent, sitting uncannily still. Gets up suddenly to make the tea, as if she knows her father is dead.

His junior school, All Saints, sandbagged above the windows, with a signboard outside saying ARP Post. His warden father takes him down there one evening, around his neck the cardboard box with his gas mask, on his head the tin hat initialled ARP. He walks beside him embarrassed along the street where they are both known, eyes on the ground. "Come and have a game of table tennis," his father has said with curious familiarity, as if they have always been on equal terms.

Standing on the old uneven boards after all this time is a weird sensation for him, trying to visualise how it had been. Stares round at the shrunken room, flaking cream distemper on the walls, the map of the world there still, spattered with red bits, the iron stove that used to be the very core of the room, the heart of his school life, his infancy, glowing, burning, a mess of coke dust around the base inside the wire cage, and he looks at it now, redundant, dead as a drainpipe. An electric fire plugged in by the side of it, where the scuttle of coke used to be. The space stripped of desks, men in rubber boots and greatcoats sitting round drinking mugs of tea, playing cards, smoking. His father greeted as Bert, hanging up his tin hat.

Confused, he struggles to adjust as he plays ping pong with his father who has changed character, bluff and slightly impersonal among the others, who dances about youthfully, all arms and legs at the other end of the table, shouting, "Wake up, dreamy! You're got a hole in yer bat, son!" It is inconceivable that this room like a barrack room was once his school.

Nights of heavy raids begin, sending them down in the Anderson and his father to the warden's post. His mother's friend from across the street, Mrs Pinches, brings over her two girls to share the shelter with them. The jollity of Mrs Pinches in all circumstances is unquenchable. Marvelling at their refuge she exclaims, "This is a bit of all right. Home from home, this is." Hessian door carefully unrolled and a candle lit. The youngest girl wants to pee, so out goes the candle and he listens to her water tinkling in the enamel chamber pot. "Is that it, Jessie?! her mother screeches. "God strewth, you've half filled the bleedin' thing." All to make them laugh.

His mother tight as a spring. Bombs whistling down. One, a few nights before, had scored a direct hit on a brick surface shelter round the corner in Gulson Road. No one knows how many killed. His mother refuses to let his father mention it. Silence, listening to the throb of German planes overhead, a sound everyone recognises as distinctive. One bomb so close it makes the earth beneath them buck like a horse. He is affected by the nervous tension but feels no fear until his mother whimpers, unable to suppress her dread. Mrs Pinches says stoutly, "Don't worry, Missus, it's them you don't hear that hit you."

He attends his first funeral. Unrecognisable in the February snow and ice is his grandmother's grave by the blotchy chapel and the ugly tree, opened to receive his grandfather's coffin. The monkey puzzle tree black and grotesque against the banked snow, the little paths around the grave buried, landmarks blotted out.

In the hired hall afterwards he is stunned by the gaiety, cold meats and hot drinks and people standing around talking and laughing uproariously, many he has not seen before; Aunt Florrie there with Fred, her high teetering laugh about to crack, Fred buttonholing anyone who will listen to his saga as he describes the journey from Leamington along atrocious roads, his car slithering sideways, even with chains, his chalk-white face excited, hands flapping. Snow falling outside the window, the topic of the roads and how to get back never ceasing.

In all the hubbub his grandfather is persona non grata, people feeding and drinking with gusto, somehow enlivened by the brush with death and with encountering each other again after years of no contact, pouring out news, spicing it with gossip. As the gathering disperses they clap each other on the shoulder, kiss and hug with unaccountable warmth. Somebody pats him on the head, a large lady, saying how he has grown. He looks in vain for signs of grief, tears, but no one cries: they have come out of duty to pay their respects and now they are happy, it is over and done. They are alive, celebrating their survival, full of energy, zestful, everyone talking at once. He averts his gaze from his mother.

Night after night now the raids intensify, his mother's nerves in shreds. One night his father is driven to give his wife some respite, sending her and his sons to stay overnight at Pinley Gardens. He is eager to go, the bungalow is on high ground and it will be a vantage point. As bombs rain down on the city centre he bolts outside before his mother can stop him, though his brother has to stay indoors. Stands on the slatted deck, the verandah a perfect viewing platform, beseeched to come in but pretending not to hear. Fires burn all over the city. He feels he has a right to be outside, fifteen years old and earning a wage, the one male as tall as a man. His other grandfather is missing, away on the railway, Cyril working nights as always. Even from this distance he can hear the frantic bells of fire engines, ambulances. When he goes in he finds his mother being consoled by his grandmother, who strokes her daughter-in-law's head with old knotted hands which have lived so long. "What about Hubert, where is he?" his mother whispers fearfully, as if frightened by her own voice, hearing her terror given words.

Wanting to go to bed, so as not to see her torment. His father walking about in the midst of fires and bells is for him indestructible because always there, every day of his life. Nothing has ever happened to him; how can it be different? Long hours on his feet at the factory have tired him, and he is soon asleep. Hears voices raised in the small hours, doors opening and shutting, silence. The anti-aircraft guns quiet. Far off, the all-clear sounding. Falls asleep again, and wakes to hear his grandmother at his bedside whispering that his mother has gone back home. Later he hears the story of her desperate search for his father, the school wall demolished, the warden's post shut down, damaged by bomb blast. Rushing up to a special constable who tells her, "If he's diseased he'll be at the mortuary," meaning deceased. Terrible to his mother's ears, but a ghoulish family joke in years to come.

So she searches like a mad thing, everywhere. Finds him at last in Coventry and Warwickshire Hospital, where his grandfather had died not long before, and where he had gone with a classmate from All Saints School carrying a basket of eggs. His father sits up in bed dazed, jaw smashed, dentures smashed, glasses smashed. Unable to speak, he puts out a hand. Alive. She grabs his live hand, sitting by his bed.

With her husband transferred to a hospital at Bromsgrove for operations, the reconstruction of his jaw and recuperation, out of reach for months, somehow the decision is taken for them to give up the rented house in Vecqueray Street and flee the nights of terror. How can his mother endure the bombing when her protector lies helpless in a hospital bed, a victim? He hears the story of how it happened, which becomes a litany when it is told repeatedly to friends and relatives, the landmine floating down horribly in a deadly silence, landing insidiously out of the black night, burying his father under the school wall. His mouth filled with rubble. Rescue workers dig him out and he gets to his feet unaided, then falls over, disorientated and in shock, blinded by dirt, unable to speak, to say who he is.

82

Aunt Florrie has told her sister of the cellar under her building in Clarendon Square that is being cleared of rubbish by the landlord for rent as a basement flat. Why not move in there, at least until Hubert comes home? Cyril is enlisted to help with the move to Leamington. Years later the elder son remembers vividly the trauma of their arrival, following her down the stone area steps into something that looks like a dungeon, conscious of his responsibility as the one grown-up male, the little surrogate husband, quailing as they descend below ground level and he sees the drooping shoulders of his defeated mother. They go down: how symbolic it is, this *down*. Is it possible to sink lower than this? Husbandless, faced with an abode like a dugout, walls of unplastered brick, draughty flagstone floors, and the smell of damp, of earth, running with insects.

In the buttressed passage is a board on the wall with a row of bells, now disused, covered in a film of dirty cobwebs. This had once been the servants' quarters, before the big house overhead was split into flats. Inside the door the gas and electric meters for the whole building, in an ugly tangle of cables high on the wall. Gas jets for lighting. A grate choked with ash that is ages old. A place to be ashamed in, a place for poor people, for refugees. This is what he sees through his mother's eyes, as she says nothing, rooted to the spot. She bursts into tears.

He has seen his mother as distraught as this only once before. In 1936 they embarked as a family on what was for him an extraordinary adventure, a camping fortnight on the Isle of Man. Their equipment had been sent on ahead in two tea chests, carefully packed and addressed to a farm outside Douglas, all arranged by his father in response to an advert in a newspaper. A car being delivered to Liverpool by his car hire firm was their free transport.

It was wonderful going over on the enormous boat, an amazing experience, climbing up into it from the quayside and then feeling it move, an utterly new sensation. But a terrible cloud descended when they found the field, advertised as near the sea but in fact three miles out of Douglas on the mountain road to Snaefell, right against the T.T. course. The field was rough and inhospitable as a common, a steep incline of poor grass, thick with thistles, all lumps. His grandmother was with them and there was no public transport. His father looked at it and said nothing, unwilling to admit to a disaster. His mother, struggling to accept, went to the farmhouse for milk and bread. A stony, slatternly woman with a withered arm opened the door, behind her a filthly kitchen. Back to his father who was busily unpacking, she said, "I can't face it, this awful place," and wept. Wounded by her heartbreak, his own heart shrank. Now, stranded in that dank cellar, he has nothing to say. Speechless, he moves further in. What has befallen them?

Yet he is astonished by his mother's resilience. By the time his father comes home, his jaw a little lopsided but otherwise fully healed, she has created a home: whitewashed the walls, scrubbed every inch of floor, hung check curtains. In no time he improves it still further, painting doors and boarding up the great iron range the servants had once cooked on, and – a master stroke – installing a slow-combustion stove, trade name *The Otto*, with a mica window which slides up to reveal the cheery glow of the coke. Every day he goes off by works bus to his progress clerk's job in the Rootes car factory at Ryton-on-Dunsmore, now devoted to war work. Splintered fragments of bone surface in his gums from time to time.

His son is the proud owner of a new Raleigh cycle with flat handlebars, and rides in to continue his apprenticeship in Coventry, ten miles each way. Soon the journey exhausts him. The Irish doctor who examines him, Miss Laverty, sends him out to sit in the waiting room while she talks to his mother. He is delighted to be given a certificate for a month off work with something called cardiac debility. Calling him back to the surgery, Miss Laverty, striding up to him on her short thick legs, says jokingly that he will live to a ripe old age unless he attempts to swim the Channel. It is a matter of simple common sense, she explains. "After all, would I dream of entering a beauty contest?" With him on one side of her and his mother on the other she puts her arms around them roughly, like a man. "She's Irish," his mother says in explanation when they are outside.

What an idyll this month at home is, for after all he is not sick, not in pain. He is supposed to rest and eat butter and eggs and drink milk, in order to build himself up, which for him is like being on holiday.

He cannot remember afterwards such a nice time. It is so easy to be slothful, to take things easy, and even easier when you are aided and abetted by your mother. Eager to make her happy in return he agrees to her every suggestion, accompanying her on walks down to the river on mellow afternoons in the still, smoky weather, going to see films which he privately thinks mushy, such as *Mrs Minniver*, calling in at the library while she chooses books like *One Pair of Hands* and *My Turn to Make the Tea* by Monica Dickens. One afternoon he paints the shutters in the living room with cream paint. If she goes shopping he goes too, though he finds it boring, carrying her basket and walking on the outside in the proper manner. He sees how his mother glows like the stove when he is attentive to her. Truly they are in accord, and he discovers how alike they are in small ways, passing comments, gossiping, exchanging little jokes. Their excursions include Northumberland Avenue, admiring the splendid houses in their own grounds and imaging what it would be like to live there, and the genteel atmosphere of the Pump Rooms, which makes him laugh because of its absurd contrast with his workaday world.

His mother insists that he stays in bed until nine, and he reads *Oliver Twist* there. It makes him enjoyably lachrymose. Along Royal Parade by himself he picks up *Bugle Blast, Modern Reading* and *Penguin New Writing*, inexpensive wartime magazines which begin to form his taste. It is a time of closeness with his mother that he somehow realises will not happen again. The tranquillity runs counter to the cold inevitability of his growing up. Saddened by this truth, which is clear to him but apparently not to her, he begins to seek more time to himself as his month of paradise comes to an end.

Chapter 13

He is aware of a secretive, consciously interior life, something to be guarded, something to steer by. His flinching exterior has this inner core which trembles in the knowledge of its arrogance. A chaste, secret grove. He is insolent with a kind of unspoken pride, a hubris, telling himself he is more alive than others because more afraid.

One afternoon his father turns up with a friend, a workmate from his office who brings his teenage daughter along. She is shy, tall, a reader like himself. He sees at once that she is a lonely creature, that they are in one sense in the same boat. Is this why she has appeared, has there been some collusion? Blushing, she holds out a collection of Chinese short stories she has brought for him to borrow, smiling in confusion at them all, avoiding his eyes. Sorry for her and for himself, more assured than her because on his own ground, he gets down his only hardback book of fiction from the shelf, *No More Mimosa*, stories by Ethel Mannin. It is his first expensive purchase, and if he is honest he does not care for it. Would she like to borrow that? She murmurs her thanks, scarcely moving her lips. Suddenly he hates this shrinking violet and wants her gone. Watches her dumbly as she departs. In a turmoil for no reason.

At work, still skinning the long steel bars, he is about to take a cut and hears a loud crack. His lathe stops working. Baffled, he stares stupidly at it. Then the belting drops from its high shaft, a lifeless snake, one end striking his shoulder. It is like being hit with a stick.

The belt is broken at the joint. The foreman spots his predicament and shouts briskly across, "Take it to be mended. Millrights, Know where they live?" He shakes his head and the foreman points, shouts, "There, up the stairs."

He is surprised by the dead weight of the belt when he carries it away. Where it passes over the pulleys the leather is rubbed smooth and glossy, quite warm. He rolls it up as small as possible and marches down the gangway self-consciously with the strange thing under his arm.

At last a more modern lathe becomes vacant and he is moved to that. It has its own motor, and a starting handle like the gear lever on a car, which he pulls towards himself with his left hand. He is conscious of his new status. He no longer has to reach over his head to shove across a shaking wooden bar, and nothing squeals when he starts up. But he is not used to the danger of so much ease of operation. One afternoon he is changing some gear wheels to begin screwcutting, and must have leaned against the rubber knob of the starting handle. His hands are among the gears, then suddenly they are moving, cogs ripping at the first three fingers of his left hand.

Somebody runs for the foreman, who grabs his coat from the wire hook on the girder and escorts him down to the works surgery. He is white at the lips, the blood dripping freely on the white lines of the gangway.

At the surgery it is decided to run him down in a van to the hospital. He sits in the front seat, feeling sick. "Here's his coat," the foreman shouts, bundling his jacket through the window. Then he is sweeping out through the gates in the quiet afternoon.

In the hospital he waits for an hour in Casualty, holding his sodden handkerchief round his wounds. It is ripped skin, but he goes home on the bus, a special case. It is mid afternoon and his mother is amazed to see him. "Where's your bike?" she asks immediately.

He describes the accident, and lifts his damaged hand. The three fingers of fat bandages burn whitely in the light. His mother looks blankly at them. "What about your bike, will it be safe there?" she asks again worriedly.

It is a disappointment, but he decides to stop being a casualty who is badly shaken. He is getting hungry. Perhaps later he will make more of an impact, when the bandages are peeled off and they see the torn flesh underneath.

Later, as he sits eating, his father comes in from work, striding in cheerfully on his long legs. He has been looking forward to his father's shocked face.

"Back early?" is all he says, not noticing.

"Look what he's done," his mother says matter-of-factly.

He explains what he has done.

"Did you write your name in the accident book?" he asks at once.

"How could he write in books?" his mother cries, not noticing which hand it is.

His hand heals quickly, leaving white rubbery unwrinkled patches on the young flesh of his fingers. Within a month there is little to see.

Now that his interest in literature has begun to give him insights into character, he studies his parents almost coldly, comparing them, trying to make sense of them. Set beside his mother, his father gives an impression of calm. He is often blithe, abstracted. It is his mother, sensitive to atmospheres and dangers, feeling unworthy, unwanted, who creates the waves of disturbance in the household. He sees it is not something she can help but he resents it. She is dark with sacrifice, burdened with love for them all. It helps to bind them to her, and burdens are piled on her because of the way she is.

In the factory he moves from section to section, absorbing different skills as best he can. At ease with none of it, going through the motions, somehow progressing through the months and years, and as if expecting to be found out. Plunging against his will into its subterranean life, one day handed a soiled pack of dirty postcards and told to pass them on. So ugly he is instantly degraded, made ill. The images burn in his hand, he stares with his whole face at the dirt done to sex, to the bodies of women. The hatred in them scalds him, he goes about feeling contaminated, even looking in the mirror to see if it shows. Stories passed round in the canteen, stained sheets stapled together, one describing the seduction of a vicar's virgin daughter. The defilement of her innocence is the triumph of the story, showing that anyone can be defiled. At the end she is a slut, gobbling at sex. Beauty is something to glamorise on the screen, and then do dirt on in private. Angels with dirty secrets.

From his basically safe town he comes and goes, sometimes getting off a bus on the edge of the bombed city and tramping down the raw swooping Fletchamstead Highway, past the ATS contingent manning the barrage balloons by a derelict farm. On the morning after the great blitz on Coventry he decides to cycle. The night before he has looked over from his aunt's flat at the sky burning, hearing on the radio later that the city is a shambles, the fires still blaze at dawn, the whole shopping district is gutted, they are still digging out bodies. He listens with strange detachment, as if he has never lived or worked there. Halfway there along the country road he comes to a road-block, police ordering him back. He hears the word corpses. He pockets his identity card and turns back his bike.

His experience of war at close quarters, when it comes, seems equally unreal. One day at the factory the sirens sing out in broad daylight before dinnertime. Men straightening up from their machines with puzzled faces. Then the machines cut dead, over his head the shafts stop twirling, the belts slow down, flap and hang quiet. This is the moment of portentous silence that the killing of the power always creates. Is it a power cut? Suddenly everyone is on the move, running madly, crouching against the blast wall built against the stores. He fails to hear the heavy pulse of the plane at first: then he hears it. Over in the far corner of the main shop there is a crash, glass dropping, somebody shouting, "All right, don't panic, he's gone now – walk out to the shelters." This is a fair distance, through the yards past the cycle racks, the cyanide and sandblasting sheds and out to brick shelters on an area of waste ground against the railway embankment. He troops along with all the others in the dull light, blinking up at the sky like everyone else.

"There the bugger is!" somebody yells. He bends double and runs the last few yards to the shelter doorway. Out of the corner of his eye he has seen it, circling slowly and banking. It seems in no hurry. Fascinated, he sees the black wing markings clearly as it makes off. In the shelter he hears some ragged machine-gun fire from the Home Guard on the top of the Standard factory roof. A week before they had let fly at a Wellington by mistake, a great joke. "See him, did you – see him?" men were exclaiming, full of wonder and admiration for the German's daring.

At the factory he has constructed a curious temporary life for himself which he half despises, mooching around the side streets at dinnertimes with a little knot of apprentices, and then when he reaches Leamington at nights and weekends his real existence takes over, when he is solitary and knows absolutely no one, and can please himself. He comes across the word autodidact and supposes he is one, widening his reading to include philosophy by popularising writers, though it bores him.

One summer he goes on holiday with four apprentices, unable to think of an excuse for not going. Someone has had the idea of hiring a boat, a yacht, where they can live on board, sleep and cook their food with no interference from adults. Somebody thinks of the Trent. In spite of his doubts he is attracted. They head for Leicester, change buses for Nottingham, then go on to Radcliffe in a taxi in grand style. As it happens he is the only one with any experience of sailing, after being taken with his brother by Cyril to the Broads years ago. He keeps quiet about this, but the others are falling over themselves to try their hand at tacking, dragging on the ropes and holding the tiller.

To his surprise he loves the feeling of freedom as they set sail for Nottingham, winding about through the dull meadows which become industrial as they draw nearer to the city. They have misadventures which are discussed with gusto later, the most serious when they nearly crash the top of the tall mast against an iron railway bridge. Lying on their bunks at night they keep roaring with laughter for no reason. It is because of the absurdity of living like this on a boat in wartime, doing idiotic things, and because they feel themselves to be freebooters. Something has happened; he is absorbed into the group and takes pleasure in being accepted. This feeling, which he has always resisted and hung back from, now seems utterly natural. The medium, by means of which he has joined them, become one of them, is humour. He can see how funny their situation is, how it is an endless source of amusement.

Things only begin to fall apart for him on their last night, when they are moored by the steps at West Bridgford. The others want to go to a dance at the Palais in Nottingham. He sits watching the intense vigour of their preparations, shoes being blacked and polished,

Brylcreem rubbed in, combs flashing, clean white shirts whipping out of the rucksacks like magic. Eddie, who is so dark that he has to shave, knocks the dandruff off his shoulders for something to do: he is raring to go. The middle button of his sports jacket is negligently fastened. Eddie, his face sore and pink, looks a dandy.

He is the only one not joining them. He is not going for the simple reason that he cannot dance. He is also virginal, and girls are a problem he has yet to confront. Instead he waves them off and passes the time by seeing a film called *Saratoga Trunk* at a cinema opposite Victoria Station. A taxi from there has been booked for eleven.

When he comes out there is still forty minutes to wait before the others turn up. It is dark, drizzling. He walks emptily in the strange dark into nowhere, heading up the hill of Mansfield Road in the warm rain. He is nowhere, nothing. Clouds of a luxurant loneliness drift through him. Goes past shops, alleys. Chemist on a corner. Church. Big hoarding at a junction. Avenue of trees and grass and a path up the middle, cutting away to the left, rising up a slope and going on, this swathe of green disappearing into the distance. It is eerie. He has nothing to do with these buildings, no connection with any of it. The street ahead goes on and on, tunnelling northwards into nowhere. People he passes have an air of menace. He reaches a park without gates, wanders in and sits on a bench. Returning down the long hill he can see the clock lit up on the station tower, some way off.

His friends turn up with a girl who stands swishing her blonde hair. She is having a lift as far as the Meadows. Eddie and the others are flushed with their triumphs in the Palais. He is glad to see them, glad his bleak vigil is over. They pile in the back of the taxi, one in front, the driver saying something in his broad Nottingham. The circuit through the town centre, skirting the empty square and shooting down narrow streets bewilders him: he is lost again.

The girl on Eddie's lap is pressed against him. "Hello, handsome," she croons, and puts her hand to his chin and strokes it, to feel the bristles. He is seventeen, not yet shaving. "Rough," the girl says softly. What he hears is an overture of love. He is struck dumb. Then she giggles and he realises his mistake. He has been examined and found wanting.

Chapter 14

Another winter. It has been snowing all night, but until he opens the door in the early morning dark and steps out, half fuddled with sleep, he has no idea. The snow creaks under his foot. He goes back in for an extra pair of socks to wear inside his gum boots. His father starts after him, catching a works bus which takes him to his factory gates at Ryton. He is up already. Walks about holding his collar; he has lost a stud. His face is bright and alert as usual. His mother fusses and grumbles, always fretful when someone is getting ready to leave. He hears his father asking again about his lost stud as he leaves the basement to tramp to the bus stop.

He is still waiting, pressed back against a wall in the Parade, when his father comes clumping up in his rubber boots which seem huge: they look twice the size of his. He tells him his works bus is not running; none of them are. He is waiting for the service one. "Where are they?" his father asks. His moustache and eyebrows have a dusting of fine snow. His cap is pulled well down.

"I haven't seen any yet."

"Let's find a doorway," he mutters, peering through his fogged glasses. The snow, after easing off, now falls as thickly as before.

His father plods over to a doorway full of glum silent men, and he has to trail after him. He is with his father but separate, and wishes he was alone as usual. He hates to see his father smiling openly at the bad-tempered faces of strangers, who refuse to budge and make room for him. Instead of giving up he stands close to them and tries to begin a conversation. All he gets is a series of grunts. His father's innocent gregariousness often embarrasses him.

He feels cold, but excitement stirs in him because of the break in routine, the question mark over the journey itself ahead of them over roads blocked with snow. They might get stuck; anything might happen. They are still in the dark, but the snow everywhere is like light.

He stands stamping his feet, aware of a growing crowd of men around them, muttering and cursing. A few cars limp past, crippled by their chains. The night over the roofs end at last. Still no sign of a bus.

Someone who has been down to the terminus at the bottom end of the town marches towards them importantly, shouting, "No buses. No buses running." Men begin scattering in all directions. He goes home again with his father. His mother's astonished face amuses him.

At ten they try a second time. There are buses now. One swings grinding round the corner and halts at their stop. It is almost full, people taking up more room with thick clothes. His father urges him on first. The only seats not taken are at the rear, under a cloud of tobacco smoke. He makes for that. He sits on an outside seat and his father takes the one behind him. They move off immediately. He listens to the crunch of chains underneath and to snatches of conversation on either side.

"They aren't supposed to put chains on buses."

"Get away?"

"Somebody was saying. If the roads are bad enough to warrant chains they shouldn't be running."

Hearing this he sits more tensely, imagining hidden dangers. They rumble and thud down the long hills and nothing happens. His hopes of a day off begin to fade, as the bus rolls forward powerfully over the slush and grit. Disappointed, he stops looking out of the window.

The conductor shoulders his way towards them past standing passengers, his face sullen. He hears voices raised in complaint as the conductor works nearer. Finally the man in front is being asked for his fare.

"Any workmen's returns?"

"Not after nine."

"I was waiting at half-past seven – where were you?"

"Not my fault."

"Not mine either."

"That's the regulation, sorry." The sullen conductor waits, with his dwindled, set face. The wallowing bus rocks him about and he straddles his legs.

"Bloody good, that's bloody marvellous," the passenger says, chewing his lips bitterly. "We haven't made the weather, you know." All at once he gives in. "How much."

His father has told him he will pay for them both, and he listens to him being asked.

"Two workmen's returns," his father says, in a peculiar, tight voice.

"Sorry, not after nine."

"Look, we got here well before that and there were no buses, and we –"

The conductor cuts him short. "Can't help that, sorry."

He looks round at his father, whose face is pink with indignation. "I want two workmen's returns," he says hotly.

"You must be deaf, Mister," the conductor says with heavy derision.

"I'm only asking for what's right," he hears his father say, then is furious and ashamed when he hears him add, "If you won't give them me, you'd better stop the bus."

He hates his father for the scene he is making, admires him for his stand and at the same time would do anything to disown him if he could.

"All the others have paid, it's just you," the conductor says.

They are glaring at each other. "What are you going to do?" his father yells, trying to make himself heard over the engine. They are roaring uphill.

"What are *you* going to do?" counters the conductor, his neck flushed. There are sniggers of laughter from somewhere.

"You can take my name and address," his father answers, suddenly dignified and calm. The battle is over. His father leans forward over the back of his seat and asks his son if he has enough money for the single ticket home in the evening. He nods miserably. He sees what a decent person his father is, a man who believes in justice, yet he cannot forgive him.

His stop is the big roundabout on the outskirts of the city, where Fletchamstead Highway meets the Kenilworth Road. He jumps up just in time, not recognising the junction at first because of the snow. He says goodbye to his father hastily and steps out, startled by the cold drenching air after the fug of the bus.

As he tramps back a few yards to the crossroads he stares at the featureless island, pure white and unmarked, the snow on the road churned into blackish mud in a circle all round it.

Setting off down the highway he is cheered by his solitary state, everyone cast off, only the sweet emptiness of the fields ahead of him. He walks loudly in his gum boots, crushing the snow and leaving large prints like a man. He enjoys wearing them, hearing the chafing sounds and lifting the unfamiliar weight each time. He feels oafish and insensitive, and that too pleases him.

No one about. The broad dual highway stretches ahead and he looks forward to the mile or so he has to travel, the vibrations of space around his head, the cold sharp on his ears, his heart lonely and bright in anticipation. He is late, so he will lose money, but the day will be short, easier to get through. He finds it better to walk in the highway itself, where the few cars have flattened the snow. At the crest of a rise he unbuttons the top of his duffle coat. His scarf is too hot round his neck, so he loosens it. The wind pushes against his back, helping him.

Tramping away with his arms swinging he relishes the sensation of freedom, the sight of his own breath on the air, the ground under his feet, the tremble of space, everything. He likes to think of himself as a transient, imagines he is a vagrant, forever moving on, different, owning nothing, forgetting that he has begun to collect books, and that he sees books as weapons to be used in some battle yet to come.

He is nearing the barrage balloon encampment and the derelict farm when he hears the car and glances sideways casually. It is already alongside, the passenger door pushed open. The driver beckons. He recognises Mr Hartley, chief engineer at the factory, a very exalted being. He has only seen him once, striding arrogantly through the office corridor as he waits at the narrow sliding window for his wage packet.

It seems incredible that this man knows him. He fully expects Mr Hartley to say he has made a mistake when he reaches the car. Instead he motions curtly to the vacant seat beside him and he gets in, mumbling his thanks. It all happens too swiftly for him to be even nervous.

They slide forward graciously, now and then rolling and sinking on the springs as if on a ship. The engineer stares through the windscreen without attempting to speak. He sits encased in absolute confidence, middle-aged, with thick skin on his cheeks and nose, and a long, slightly turned-down mouth, his large hands steering them clad in soft, expensive-looking dark gloves.

He remembers the odour of suds oil clinging to his clothes, though when he tries to smell it he cannot. He fears he may have grown used to it. In the mornings when he pulls on his trousers it is always strong.

They lift over the railway bridge and sink down on the other side. In no time they are at the gates, swinging in, and he sees the yellow-faced police sergeant touch his peaked cap to them, then walk back to his blockhouse.

The car halts outside the wide-open mouth of the works entrance. In there, lights blazing down, the morning well advanced, people walking about busily. When he finds the right lever and opens the door he hears the complex humming and clapping from everything, the medley of motors, belts and shafting.

"Thank you very much," he calls in a stilted voice to the assured, remote figure seated behind the wheel. Mr Hartley gives an almost imperceptible nod without turning his head. Meekly he shuts the door and leaves him to glide away like a ghost.

Though he resents having his walk curtailed it is a relief to escape the rarified atmosphere inside the car. For once he is glad to be there, to march under the dangling hoist past the litter of packing stuff round the scales and go into the noisy shop where he belongs.

Chapter 15

Nearly eighteen, he is on the look-out for special people, as he will be soon for dead artist-heroes, men whose way seems to be the way of brokenness, who triumph after their death, like van Gogh, for instance. Investing them with glory binds them to him in some way he does not understand. It is an act of love that has no repercussions, that makes no demands. It could be said that he is in search of spirit fathers, except that he has no belief in spirits. The dead god he has pretended to worship at Sunday School has not really touched him. He is unaware that a boy of eighteen in paroxysms of adoration for an unapproachable shining figure who is essentially flawless, pure, raised up, is not exactly uncommon.

Flesh and blood heroes, people he can see if not touch, are not so easy to find. They have to be doing something that no one else can possibly do as well, to be in fact crowned for the job. Stan Boult has this aura for him. During the six months he is on the fitters' benches of Precision Instruments, filing away at some menial task and flicking glances in his direction, he has eyes only for him. How can he be sure that this person is so extraordinary? But the question does not enter his head. When his hero is missing for a day he is downcast, his own day under a cloud.

Stan Boult, a young, fair, slender man with a wisp of fair moustache, is in his eyes an aristocrat among toolmakers. One can tell this by his disdainful gesture, his discreet asides to a friend, above all by his gentle, courteous treatment of his boss, a big snowy-headed old veteran whose limbs are in soft fat curves, his face florid like a retired sea captain. Mr Saunders affects a tough, gruff exterior to compensate for the fact that his powers have waned, and now he defers obsequiously to his star fitter, this young man of superior skill who is given the most complex tasks, intricate assemblies to be built up.

His secret admirer sees Stan Boult as uniquely gifted, his long fingers probing the innards of instruments with the delicacy of a surgeon, intuitive in his response to the messages of his brain. His boss acknowledges all this by allowing him endless time, asking advice about solutions to near insoluble problems. "How's it going, Stan?" he asks, waiting obediently for a sign, satisfied with a shake of the head, his power usurped. In return he is treated with tender consideration and with proper respect for his age, for the years of experience accumulated in the old, defeated body. Too far away to hear their exchanges, the apprentice sees the working of his hero's throat and imagines the rest, thrilled by the obvious subtlety of his whole being. He will never be disillusioned by close contact, faults of character, pettiness, ugly comments.

When he is moved to another section, Stan Boult continues to live in him as a man without flaw, someone he enshrines in his interior life, glorifies in his beauty and potency like a god. With such attributes he dreams of being lordly and proud himself one day, instead of always in knots of shyness and inadequacy, and with no skill worth mentioning, forever fumbling and unsure, crippled by a chronic lack of confidence. Stan Boult is a kind of icon, a key to a life that yet might be, where he saunters at ease, walks with grace and inspires devotion in his turn.

A very different kind of hero who infatuates him for a time is a young man in his twenties he only knows as Bob. As with Stan Boult, he is in no position to exchange a word with him, so that again the disillusionment that comes with familiarity is spared him. This time the potency and beauty that casts its spell on him is purely physical. He watches Bob purely in terms of his body, loving his irresistible charm and zest, his wide grin, broad shoulders and narrow hips, breasting along so zippy and eager. Bob is the craggy open-air type, ready to talk football any time, the kind of person he has absolutely nothing in common with. Having no idea what Bob is really like he invests him with qualities, imagining him to be like a gentle, intelligent, laughing boxer.

Down in the club room under the canteen at dinnertimes he is the ardent spectator, sitting to watch Bob competing in table tennis matches. His vigorous crisp returns and the habit he has of letting himself be forced back and back, crouching, fighting a defensive battle, captivates him far more than if he had been winning. He derives endless pleasure from studying his stance, his swift lunges, hearing his yells of triumph, even the boastful way he struts about. The whole point of a hero is that he can do no wrong.

What a contrast is Clarrie Noy, a boy of his own age whose name strikes him as funny, who has an oddly-pitched high voice, but who possesses a curious intensity which he admires in spite of himself. And for all his oddity, this fellow apprentice with his white intense little face, his fixed stare, his passionate, fanatical torrents of verbiage, does have a touch of something almost heroic about him. A glance as he passes Clarrie at work on his big milling machine puts them in touch, a look that both pleads and challenges, that asks: Are you my audience?

In an incongruous setting, machines howling around them and a prowling foreman eyeing them beadily, he hears of Clarrie's ambition to turn himself into a playwright. Soon he tires of being subjected to this one unstoppable desire, but unless he takes a different route to the stores there is no way he can avoid him. If he is truthful he is at first fascinated and sympathetic, but before long he feels worn down by the sheer absurdity of Clarrie's impossible dream. Why he finds him absurd he would find it hard to say. Chiefly it is his manner. All he has to show by way of encouragement is some sporadic correspondence with an agony aunt on the *Daily Mail*, to whom he has sent one of his scripts.

"Remind me to bring you her letter," he gabbles, as the foreman edges nearer, about to send him back to his own section. "See this, look at this," he cries, brandishing a feature on Peter Ustinov, prodigy at eighteen, posed in his white open shirt and clever toothy smile, toast of the West End. "If he can do it, why not me?"

His idols spilling out, Chekhov, Strindberg, above all the greatest, Ibsen, a master of symbolism. And then his own work in progress.

Every night at home tearing into it, locked away in a box room with a chair and trestle table, to the consternation of his bewildered loving parents. "They haven't a clue, they think I'm about to have a breakdown but they love me – what more could I ask?"

Spying him trying to sneak by, Clarrie flags him over, protruberant eyes wild with zeal, burning to expound on the symbolism of *The Wild Duck*, losing him completely though he nods away, impressed yet again by Clarrie's drive, his furious ambition. He has finished one play of three acts and is roughing out another. "I'll get there, nobody's going to stop me, it's a matter of belief," he explains with fervour. "If you want something badly enough, hard enough, you get it." Getting his analysis of Ibsen and his dream of success out in one continuous stream, angry and agitated, mad with impatience.

Unlike Clarrie he knows nothing of modern theatre, only names, yet discovers in himself an irrational scepticism with regard to drama, a resistance he cannot explain. He keeps these reservations to himself, for he can imagine Clarrie's derision. A young man a few years older than himself, John Preston, is also interested in the theatre, but has decided he is worth cultivating because he seems bookish. Certainly he now reads voraciously, and John Preston comes visiting across the shop floor to where he now stands working a surface grinder. Tall and handsome, rather languid, middle-class, he enjoys being told about likes and dislikes. "You don't say," he drawls. "How interesting. I must have another look at him." He is flattered, though he thinks it weird that John Preston should come for guidance to him for his choice of reading, when the truth is that he knows next to nothing, he is just following his nose.

He has no political discussions with Preston, their common ground is only books, so he is bemused when he sees this cordial, elegant, rather wishy-washy young man in strange alliance with Alec Jenkins the works convenor. When Jenkins holds his dinner-hour seminar on Marxism and the role of the union movement on the grass verge of the highway, a little group of followers around him, John Preston is there with a bundle of *Daily Workers* and a tin mug for a collection in aid of the paper's Fighting Fund. Alec is rumoured to be a dedicated Communist, and he can believe it. A small, middle-aged man with a gritty bitten-off speech, with cold twinkling blue eyes and a bitter relish for the class war, he operates a shuddering planer so massive that it dwarfs him. He stands against the huge table sliding back and forth, tapping the tool over another fraction of a turn, and the cast iron sprays off the raw strapped-down casting in a rasping fountain of hot chips. His hands permanently black from the iron dust, he can be seen marching through the shop on his way to confront the management, bow-legged, a charred, indomitable figure, a bit of black moustache over his lip as if the back of his hand had smudged it on.

He belongs to the old school, and so does Bill Ogden, a veteran skilled turner who befriended him a year ago and whom he now does his best to avoid. He has made the mistake of showing sympathy for this man he has seen working without pause in his effort to make his piece-work rates pay, his face tense with effort, winding up the saddle towards the great hoops of iron with one hand while he gives the tool turret a final yank with his wrench. Too late he pauses to pass the time of day with this man lowering his cindery hard head, realising at once by his bitter, sore eyes and ravaged face, before he even speaks, that he has a grudge, he is being cheated, and the injustice he complains about is eating him alive. If he pauses, wiping his hands on a wad of cotton waste, it is only for a matter of seconds, his smile like a rat-trap, gleaming and ferocious. Bill's buttonholing approach to conversation is, he understands, an aspect of his possessiveness. And he suspects rejection. His eyes bore into him and there is no escape. He has a disconcerting habit of shooting out personal direct questions, while saying nothing whatsoever about himself. "What's new, then? What you got to tell me, eh?"

"Oh nothing ... nothing much."

"Must be something, eh?"

"Can't think what."

"Dad okay? Your mother?"

"Fine ..."

"How old's your father, eh? Old as me?"

Now he avoids him, hating the thwarted fury of his contorted face, and dreads meeting him by accident at the stores.

His lack of a girl friend, confronted as he is by fellow apprentices who seem to have no problems in this department, has begun to haunt him. In other ways he has taken care to behave like everyone else. In a moment of panic he decides to force the issue, passing a note to Sylvia, a stocky little typist he has spotted in the Wages Office and on her jaunty promenades every two or three days across the shop floor. He is not in the least attracted to this girl, and in his heart he knows the exercise is bound to fail. But the problem nags at him now all the time, and he longs for some peace of mind.

He watches her passage through the thickets of machines and flapping belts with frightened eyes. Not that he is afraid of her – it is the action he contemplates. Her appearance never changes: a white shirt-blouse, high lacy collar, a springy bubble-cut hair-do, her eyes firmly downcast to ward off the wolf whistles.

He enlists the help of Doreen on the capstans, giving her a note which she is willing to deliver, loving her mission. Soon she is back with an answer, his own note with one word scrawled across it: Yes. Be on the corner of Torrington Avenue at dinnertime, he is told, and a time.

Close up she is somehow different, walking up to him with that bouncy little walk. She has the hint of a cast in one eye. "How did you know my name?" she wants to know at once.

"Oh, somebody told me."

"Somebody I know?"

He shakes his head dumbly.

Near the gates he forces out his request for a date.

"When?"

"Thursday night?"

"I can't Thursday," she says coyly, with a slyness he hates.

"Friday, then."

Again the little catlike smile. "What time?"

Inside, he stands at his machine telling himself that the deed is done, feeling he has paid in blood. His head bent to the task, he begins to exult. What lies ahead is nothing, a foregone conclusion, he tells himself. He is quite prepared for a disaster. But the insurmountable barrier has been overcome, one he had thought utterly impossible.

That is the amazing thing. He wonders at the subterfuge of his act, and whether his smile of triumph looks as indecent as it feels.

He has arranged to meet her at the Gaumont, the cinema of her choice. They are showing *Samson and Delilah*. He thinks this Hollywood version of the story ridiculous, and barely conceals his dislike of Victor Mature with his greasy good looks, his swollen mouth. He is glad to be out in the evening streets, escorting her home to Barrass Lane, the experiment nearly over. Their conversation is stilted, mainly because of his ineptitude. Under the street lamps as he approaches her house he sees her small lifted face, smooth and complacent.

The film has prompted her to consider her mortality. He feels sudden pity for her when she says, in a simple child's voice, "Sometimes, when I think I've got to die, I wish I'd never been born."

"Don't you believe in heaven?" he asks, joking.

She shakes her head. In an instant her mood changes and she asks if he ever goes to dances. He tells her he has never learnt.

They have come to a halt. "Do you object to girls going in pubs?" she asks abruptly and comically.

"I don't think so."

She lights a cigarette. "I'm a shocking chain-smoker," she confesses. "I get through pounds and pounds." Suddenly she looks directly into his face. "You're very serious, aren't you?" she says curiously. "Are you self-conscious?"

The empty question floors him utterly, since there is no escape from its truth. Hatred floods into his heart. He says vaguely that he will be in touch and makes his escape.

He has to run to the bus station, scrambling on the last bus to Leamington. Sitting against the window, staring out at the blacked-out streets, he condemns himself for his self-betrayal, for the exposure. He feels like a creature dragged naked out of its shell, and the dreadful image makes him itch about on his seat. Instead of remaining true to his nature, which is to be as inconspicuous as possible, he has done the opposite, putting himself with ridiculous solemnity through this trial, this meaningless ordeal. By the time he reaches his stop he has recalled in meticulous detail each moment of humiliation, each pang of shame. Telling himself it is only hurt pride does nothing to reduce the pain.

He goes in, with nothing to say, and his mother reads the whole story in his eyes. His stiff, bitter face is more than she can bear. "What a problem you are," she says softly in reproach.

"Why should I be?" he says furiously. "You make a problem when there isn't one. Why do I have to be the same as other sons? Is that what you want?"

"No," she says, and seems to wilt in her chair.

Chapter 16

His brother, a grammar school boy, obtains a position at the Council House in Coventry, a local government officer in the making. They move back as a family to their native city as the war ends, to a semi-detached war-damaged house that feels luxurious, with its long rear garden and an actual bathroom. The years of war work have made his father almost prosperous for the first time in his life. The cul-de-sac, called Bassett Road, is in Coundon, worlds away from the inner city streets of his childhood. Somehow though, the trim respectability of its bay windows and privet hedges lowers his spirits. He prefers the basement they have vacated.

He is near the end of his apprenticeship, and often finds himself biking home with Vincent, an apprentice fitter a year or two younger who lives a few streets away in the same district, in a large detached house with affluent parents. Vincent enjoys what he calls the other's cynicism. He is amused by this, but finds it flattering. They have little in common, and Vincent's tough exterior and his jeering indifference do not deceive him. Underneath he is sentimental, an overgrown baby. He finds Vincent easier to take when he is with his girl Francie, a young red-head he is courting, a shrewd girl who acts sometimes as Vincent's stooge, swopping wisecrack for wisecrack, but under it all is not taken in. He sees them quarrelling once in the road: she has been kept waiting for half an hour. "You're late," she says, and before Vincent can open his mouth she flounces off, white-faced, furious. He looks crestfallen, a fool.

Vincent and Francie visit him one Saturday afternoon in his front room. Vincent has brought along a favourite record, Stan Kenton's *Peanut Vendor* – Vincent is mad on American big bands. The deafening crescendo mounts and he wonders how much more he can stand of the frenzied riffs, as the bass riots. All at once he grasps the reason for the wild chaos of sound: this is a machine-age rhapsody. Vincent, who has heard it a dozen times and is only half listening, nibbles boyishly at his girl's neck and says in a stage whisper, winking in his direction, "Let's go snogging tonight." Francie rebukes him with a freezing glare: "Don't say that word, it's horrible!"

The first bitter winter after the end of the war threatens to bring the whole country to a halt. "We're bankrupt," he hears his father say. In the factory the heating has been drastically reduced. Men are working with woollen gloves on. Power cuts are a regular occurrence, and then one afternoon all the machinery goes dead, and rumour has it that a substation has exploded. Men stand about in confusion, with no information from the management. After half an hour the trickle of deserters has become a stream. He stamps his frozen feet and heads for the bike sheds, on his way home like the others. Some are clocking off, so he does the same.

At home, his mother is at the kitchen table, which has been dragged away from the wall. She stands ironing, taking long hasty strokes, her face red. A half-loaded clothes horse gapes open, nearly as tall as her, scenting the warm air. She looks up, surprised to see him.

"Power gone. Shut down," he says, fumbling with his buttons.

"Isn't it dreadful, you look frozen stiff – go and sit by the fire. I'll bring you a hot drink – what did you say?" she says, all in one breath and scarely looking up, her iron shooting across.

"Broken down," he shouts through from the living room.

"What is?"

"The factory."

"Oh, is it?"

Blowing on dead fingers, listening to the rubbing and bumping. She calls, "I shouldn't go too near that fire, you'll get hot-aches." He has heard this all through his childhood.

Later, thawing out and with the use of his fingers, he sits swallowing the tea, sinking his nose over the steam as she comes struggling in with the laden clothes-horse. He gets up. "Give it to me."

"Careful," she warns.

"Where do you want it? How near?"

He sets it round the fire. She comes to inspect it. "Men have no idea," she grumbles mildly. He has heard this for years too. "There, that should do. Now you can watch it for me."

She hurries away, back to the kitchen to clear up and begin something else. He hears the rattle of saucepans.

After a few minutes he is bored. Gets up, runs upstairs to find a book. He sits on the cold bed with it a moment, turning the pages. Then a terrible cry from his mother below fills the house with horror. "Oh God, oh God, quick, quick!" she is shrieking.

The fear rushes through his veins, drives him out of the bedroom, carries him along blindly. He cannot remember later going downstairs. His mother stands in the hall coughing, her eyes terrified. Even then the smell conveys nothing. She holds a bundle of smouldering linen away from her, between her hands.

"In there – it's on fire – open the kitchen door – oh God no, don't go in, I don't want you to go in, I don't want anyone else to touch it!" she screams, blundering past him into the frozen yard. He stares horrified at the sight of her awful, stricken face.

In the living room it is dark as night, full of dense, slowly-rolling brown smoke. At the far side, where the fireplace is blotted out, he can see a big dimly glowing mass. The terrifying stench is like that of rags burning on a refuse tip. Trembling with shock he gropes in and locates the clothes-horse.

He snatches things off, ruined shirts and vests, teacloths, towels, and rushes into the yard. Running down the path to the frozen garden he tries to dig snow off the flower beds with his fingers but it is all congealed and useless.

He rushes distractedly to and fro with burnt garments. Each time he passes his mother she moans, "Couldn't you smell it? Surely you must have been able to smell it?"

He is afraid of her. He has never seen her like this. She seems a long way off, buried in her racking distress, trampled on and broken, wailing in anguish, and she is looking right through him.

The wind has dropped. He fills a bowl with water and douses the charred, smoking heap of washing. There is a loud hiss, steam rising dismally in a slow cloud, hanging over the ground.

"House ruined ... all the clothes ... room just decorated ... the soot. I wish I was dead." His mother keeps wandering up and down, unable to keep still, dragging at her apron with convulsive movements. She cries weakly, with wide-staring eyes. He stands helpless, sick with guilt and misery.

"I thought you were in the room, watching," she quavers. Her crying stops, and she seems to come back. "Where did you go?" she asks, almost in a normal voice.

He touches her fearfully. "Come in the kitchen, in the warm."

"No, no – leave me alone!" she breaks out, wailing again. She covers her face. Her hair all loose. Hysterical, with queer sounds shaking out of her.

The winter sun begins to sink, red but icy. By the time Cyril calls in, his mother is slumped in a kitchen chair exhausted, her expression quite blank and dead. His uncle bends over with his worried face and shy hands, a good man, smelling of the cold. "Any brandy?" Cyril asks him softly. He moves to look, but his mother is moving her head and trying to speak. "No," she whispers.

He follows his uncle inside to survey the damage. One layer of clothes is completely ruined, but when the smoke clears through the opened window the room itself seems remarkably unharmed. There are no marks on the ceiling. The hearth rug has a large hole eaten from the middle, where a burning tablecloth has dropped down.

When his father comes in from work he goes about saying repeatedly in a dogged refrain, "It might have been much worse."

In the days that follow his mother's breakdown – this is how he describes it to himself – he discovers that his feelings towards her have altered profoundly. The near calamity, for which he was at least partly responsible, forces him to acknowledge what he and his mother have always done to each other. Now he shrinks back from her with a suspicion that he is inwardly damaged, and by a process which has been going on for as long as he can remember. Her wild grief, out of all proportion to the event, all but turned the world black, as black as that room, robbing him of the will to live. He is being taught by this accident and its aftermath that his mother is the problem, rather than himself. Once and for all he believes he understands, and in so doing rejects something in which he has unconsciously been complicit. In future his love for her will be a wary love. Her shy, hiding expression in photographs tells it all, his story as well as her own. In these snapshots he stares at a feminine version of his own secret face.

He comes home one evening to find his brother in the front room with a friend, Ron Hall. They are of the same age, and work together in the ancient Council House in Broadgate. The strange boy, brown eyes and fair hair, small beautiful hands, touches the books in his bookcase respectfully, awestruck. "Haven't seen so many books," Ron says jokily, but means it.

'Don't know how they all got there," he jokes back, and in a flash their mutual destiny is established. He seems to sense that this boy will be immensely important to him, though he is unformed, gauche, and for some time will regard him as knowledgeable because older, foolish though he knows this to be. But he can almost hear the thoughts buzzing in this young newcomer's head, and what he loves at once is Ron's gift of recognition. His gaze swoops into him, recognising a buried self, hiding like his own.

His father is a glazier, subject to spells of mental illness, his mother semi-literate, their home poor, scrubbed clean, up a rising barren street in Hillfields, occupied long ago by watchmakers who had workshops in the attics. Behind the terraced house is a court, four privies back to back, like the slums in Much Park Street where his mother grew up. He and Ron take it in turns to play records in each other's front rooms, and one Sunday he is formally invited to his new friend's house in Vernon Street for tea. The family live in the back, as his did in Vecqueray Street. Ron's mother is short, her broad plump shoulders beginning to hunch. As well as Ron there are two younger brothers. His mother's pale, puffy face is selfless, her arms energetic. She lives in her apron, sleeves always rolled up, and nearly shouts with an energy that is half anxiety. Tea is tinned fruit, followed by a mound of pink jelly annointed with condensed milk, and bread and butter with it, the staple diet, the filler. Not joining them at the table is Ron's father, a small, weathered, intensely silent man in the corner, watchful but usurped.

Ron Hall, quick, small, brown, a scholarship boy, one of only six in Coventry to go on to King Henry's. His impish brightness lights up the room. Very cleverly he ingratiates himself with his new friend's mother, intrigued when he hears her upstairs in the boxroom typing a letter on her old machine. "What is she doing?" Ron asks politely.

"Trying to write a novel," he jokes, and for a moment he is believed.

As week follows week, Ron attaches himself to both him and his brother as they discover Sibelius, Beethoven and the jubilant Armstrong on records, his brother sitting there in his extraordinary sealed silence. Then it becomes clear that his brother is disengaging himself and Ron is connected to him alone, as if to some vision of a life that will one day transform him.

Ron is fascinated by their piano, by its possibilities, asking one day what was being played as he came in. "Oh, just something I made up." Ron nods, leaning forward receptively, eager to discover riches, marvels, asking to hear it again; so he repeats the lame, halting, meagre little tune. They treat each other tenderly, gently, with an endless flow of easy humour. They are attentive, always sympathetic. This is the honeymoon of their relationship.

So it begins, a friendship to change the course of his life. He is seen heroically, and how absurd that is, until he finds himself striving to be the strong purposeful figure he is already in Ron's eyes. As he allows this persona to be projected on him, so he projects on Ron an image of his friend as a being who is swift and bright and daring, eager to embrace life as he longs to do and cannot. In his friend's magical presence he is speechless no more. Indeed, he astonishes himself with his own eloquence. The words pour from him; he can talk, talk.

Soon now he will meet another stranger, a woman who takes his hand suddenly and squeezes. Boldness and intimacy like a thunderclap, a cloudburst, his tremulous blood in contact at last – lost in the Nottingham night of bare trees in November, devoured by a hunger for love, perhaps in love with his own youth. Thin and grateful, by the black river. The women's inspired move his undoing. She could be fifteen years his senior: poor skin, chin small and pointed. A mother. In the cold and fog his initiation begins.

Shoestring Press also publish the following books by Philip Callow.

BLACK RAINBOW: a novel, 1999 £6.99 paperback original. "Highly recommended", *Private Eye*.

TESTIMONIES: NEW AND SELECTED POEMS, 2000, £8.95. "His poems are fresh, honest and alive — and not ashamed to be so." Jeremy Robson, *Tribune*.

Shoestring Press also publish the following books by Philip Callow.

BLACK RAINBOW: a novel, 1999 £6.99 paperback original. "Highly recommended", *Private Eye.*

TESTIMONIES: NEW AND SELECTED POEMS, 2000, £8.95. "His poems are fresh, honest and alive — and not ashamed to be so." Jeremy Robson, *Tribune.*